# WHITE PAGES

© 2016, 2019 Randolph Walker, Jr.
Cover image used courtesy of Gavin Allanwood

10 9 8 7 6 5 4 3 2

ISBN 9781020001031

45 Alternate Press, LLC
Hampton, Virginia

# WHITE PAGES

RAN WALKER

*For Mom*

1

---

Kamal Jackson sat at a small table near the front of Nell's Bookstore, a small stack of his latest novel, *A Junkyard of Absurdities*, resting in front of him—just enough copies to be respectful of the fact he had taken the subway across town to be the last author in the Soul Spot reading series. When he had arrived an hour earlier, one of the sales associates, a self-proclaimed fan, let it slip that his book had not sold many copies since it first appeared on the shelves a year earlier. "I just don't get it," the fro-hawked, bespectacled guy offered. "This is the kind of book that should be selling like hotcakes. It's like a blerd manifesto!" Kamal had nodded his thanks, but quietly wondered just how few copies had actually sold.

An hour into his "signing" he realized the kid might have been generous in his earlier assessment. Since the event had begun, ten people had come into the store and glanced uncomfortably in his direction before slinking away to other parts of the bookstore.

"We might want to go ahead and get started with the reading, if you still want to do it," the store manager said. She was a polite dreadlocked woman who reminded him a lot of his Aunt Violet, a woman who rarely wore a fabric that had not been imported from the Motherland.

Kamal glanced around at the nearly empty store and slowly rose from his chair, stretching his legs. The manager escorted him to the stage-like platform at the back of the store, where they had placed a lectern with an unnecessary microphone threaded through the adjustable snake-like microphone holder. The place was small enough that he could have spoken in a conversational tone and still have had his voice fill the room. That is how he learned the two person staff had had some trouble interesting the handful of wandering customers in meeting the author seated near the front, the eager guy itching to remove the cap of his new Montblanc in hopes of signing his first autograph of the year.

By the time Kamal organized his book and reading glasses on the lectern, he realized he was about to read to a virtually empty store. The store manager and the bespectacled kid sat on opposite sides of the twenty seat arrangement in a weak effort to make themselves look like a crowd. In the back corner, seated with his fingers interlocked across his belly, sat an older bald guy, shades covering his eyes. Kamal didn't know if the guy was even awake.

He thumbed through his book, searching for the section he'd planned to read. "Well, I'd like to thank all of you for coming out this Saturday afternoon," Kamal started.

The bespectacled kid laughed aloud for a moment, thinking the comment a joke, before sliding down into his seat with one finger raised, Baptist-style, asking to be excused for his faux pas.

Kamal offered a weak smile to assuage the kid's concerns before continuing. "Did anyone have any special requests?" He held up his book, this time making a joke—one that fell flat. "I guess I'll just read what I had planned to read."

His last few readings had not gone much better than this one. The attendance was thin, the audience apathetic. At one of those earlier readings he had almost muttered, "Fuck it," into the microphone and begun ripping pages from his book. The only reason he hadn't done it was because his literary agent, Vanessa Travont, had been in the audience, seated in the second row, and she would have never let him live it down if he had done it. But Vanessa was not here today, as she had stopped attending his events, although this one was technically in her neighborhood, roughly seven blocks from her office. *Maybe I* will *just rip out the pages of my life in front of these three people and leave out of here unburdened of poor sales and industry disregard and start a new career vlogging about cats*, he thought.

Kamal cleared his throat and adjusted his glasses. Just then the door at the front of the store opened and in trotted Twan Gates, impeccably dressed, as usual, his smile broad, arms lifted high, waving enthusiastically. Standing next to him was a petite woman rocking bantu knots and shades like Jada Pinkett-Smith from that *Matrix* sequel. She was fly in a way that suggested she had come from the same gene pool as Twan. This must have been the cousin Twan had mentioned would be coming to stay with him for the summer.

Kamal nodded in their direction, relieved to see at least one face he recognized. He looked down at the book in front of him, leaned closer to the microphone (hell, it was there to be used, so he would use it), and allowed his voice to fill the small space for the next ten minutes.

---

KAMAL SAT ACROSS FROM TWAN AND YASMIN, THE mystery woman with the shades. She had been the only person to purchase one of his books, which, incidentally, offered him the sole use of his Montblanc. They had adjourned to a coffee shop several blocks from Nell's Bookstore.

"I can't begin to tell you how relieved I was to see you two come through that door," Kamal said.

"You know I got your back," Twan said, his voice animated and warm. "James would have been there, but you know he's an understudy at that new play downtown. He told me to make sure I showed up to represent for both of us."

"Well, I appreciate it. Seriously."

"Hey, for the people who didn't show up, it was their loss. You were dope," Yasmin offered.

Kamal allowed her compliment to wash over him, as he was in desperate need of one. "Thank you."

"Yasmin wanted me to bring her up here when I told her I was coming," Twan said.

"Really?"

Yasmin nodded. "I'm a fan," she offered, unable to conceal her smile. "Your first novel, *Dope Revolution*, is a classic! If I had known that Twan knew you, I would've brought my copy from Memphis."

"You have my first novel? So that explains the one sale I got from Tennessee."

Yasmin laughed loudly, as if Kamal had told the mother of all jokes.

"Damn, girl," Twan said, smiling. "I can't take yo country ass nowhere."

Yasmin continued to giggle, this time covering her mouth.

"Don't cover your smile," Kamal said. "I like it."

Twan lifted an eyebrow. "All right. I see where this is going. I'm the third wheel now, right?"

"It's all love, cuz," Yasmin said, laying her head on Twan's shoulder.

"Yeah, right," Twan responded.

"So what do you guys have planned for later?" Kamal asked.

"Well, I'm supposed to meet up with James after his show. I don't know what Yaz has planned, though." Twan playfully nudged his cousin.

Taking his cue, Kamal said, "Yasmin, would you like to get a bite to eat this evening?"

"Sure."

"Well, we can all take a cab down to James's show and just break out from there," Kamal said.

"I'm good with that, if Yaz is."

"That's cool. I'll call you if anything comes up," she said.

"All right, cuz. But you're in good hands." Twan turned toward Kamal. "Isn't that right, Kamal?"

"Most definitely. I won't let anything happen to her."

"I know," Twan responded. "But don't get it twisted, Kamal. My little cuz can take care of herself, too."

Kamal did not know exactly what Twan meant, but he caught a glimpse of Yasmin's bantu knots and shades, now resting on her forehead, and thought about Jada Pinkett-Smith kicking ass within The Matrix. He smiled.

"Let's go ahead and get that cab," Twan said. "I don't want to keep James waiting."

Kamal nodded, making eye contact with a smiling Yasmin. He didn't want Twan to keep James waiting either.

## 2

"So what brings you to The City?" Kamal asked, as he and Yasmin sat on a bench facing the river, the sun setting against an orange and violet horizon.

"I just needed something different."

"Different from Memphis?"

"Yeah," she responded, gazing at the water. "I majored in music at Lemoyne-Owen. Ended up teaching piano and voice in an after-school program, while singing background for this local wedding band. When Twan told me to come up here and check things out for a while, I figured it couldn't hurt."

"Kudos for taking the leap," Kamal said.

Yasmin nodded. "You're not from here either, are you?"

"Mississippi, born and bred."

"What part?"

"Northeast, a small town named Daily. It's about forty-five miles south of Tupelo."

"That's not too far from Memphis, is it?"

"Not at all," Kamal said.

"So you can relate to my situation then," Yasmin said.

"No doubt. I came here because I figured this is where serious writers came when they wanted to make something happen."

"That's what I want for my music career. Twan told me that I would be a fool if I didn't at least try it out. James even agreed to set up a meeting for me with his agent to see if I can get a few auditions for shows around town."

"So you act, too?"

"I do everything I can. A sista has got to be multi-talented these days to get a job."

"I feel you. When I came here, I was cobbling to-gether a living by freelancing and living off student loans from grad school. You just have to do what you have to do to give yourself a chance to succeed."

"Well, it definitely worked for you," Yasmin said.

"What do you mean?"

"You're successful. It worked!"

Kamal chuckled and looked away. "Did you see how empty that store was? That's not being successful."

"So what if one bookstore has a low turnout for one of your readings? There're a lot of people who love your work, just like I do. They just couldn't get to Nell's today to show you. That's all."

"I appreciate your words. Really, I do. It's just a little bit more complicated than that."

"How so?"

"Well, for starters, my literary agent didn't even bother walking the few blocks to support me at my reading."

Yasmin shrugged. "That has more to do with your agent than with you."

"Maybe. I don't know. I mean, I'm two books in and still trying to recoup my original advance. It wouldn't surprise me if my publisher shot me the deuces."

"This is The City. If that happens, just get a new publisher."

"Easier said than done. They all check your Book-Scan numbers to see what your sales are like before they sign you. I would almost be better off starting over publishing under a new name," Kamal said.

"I'm sure it's not that bad."

Kamal sighed and shrugged his shoulders. "Well, I'll find out sooner or later. But enough of my depressing career. Are you excited about meeting James's agent?"

"You're lucky I like you," Yasmin said.

"Why do you say that?"

"You can't just switch topics like that on a sista."

"Well, I didn't want to bring down the mood."

"We're just having an honest conversation. One day I might need your shoulder to lean on, so I would hope you'd be able to do the same."

"Right." Kamal cast his gaze at the faint remnants of the sun out ahead of them. "I see why you're Twan's favorite cousin."

"How did you know I was his favorite cousin?" Yasmin asked.

"Well, I know Twan doesn't open up his place to just anyone. But beyond that, I know my roommate pretty well. James mentioned you were coming, just like I'm sure Twan wanted to make sure we met and had a chance to spend some time together."

"I told him I wanted to meet you," Yasmin said.

"I'm glad you did."

Yasmin smiled and laid her head on Kamal's shoulder. "I love the skyline here. It's all so beautiful. I never thought I would be here—staying here—and seeing all of this with my own eyes."

"It looks better than it does on TV," Kamal added.

"Yeah, it does."

"It kind of reminds me of all of the possibilities that exist out there. That's one of the reasons I like to come here. This place and most bookstores are my sanctuaries. I guess that's why I keep writing. I keep thinking the next book will be better, more successful, and one day people will read my words long after I'm gone and say to themselves, 'Damn, that brotha really put it down!'"

"Nice," Yasmin responded. "But just so you know, you don't have to be dead and gone or even wait years for that to happen. I can tell you now, unequivocally, that you, my brotha, have put it down!"

Kamal smiled. He turned his head and planted a soft kiss against Yasmin's temple and gently laid his head against hers.

3

Vanessa Travont's office was located on the third floor of a brownstone in the Arts District of The City, neatly tucked away at the end of the hall. When she had first signed Kamal, he'd spent many hours lounging around her office, just happy to be in the mix of things. Vanessa had numerous pictures of her more famous clients on the walls, stacks of their bestselling books piled in various corners of the room. Kamal would daydream as he sat in one of her office swivel chairs, imagining a small stack of his own books cluttering her floor, as well.

Vanessa had fed his daydreams, gassing him up about his writing. She had discovered him through a short story that had been published in an anthology edited by one of her authors. From there she rolled out the red carpet, encouraging him every step of the way toward the completion of his first novel. The book sold shortly afterwards, and he assumed he was on his way to a strong career as a writer. Three and a half years later, however, he was still a long way from recouping the advances on either of his two novels.

When Kamal reached the second floor, he noticed her office door was slightly ajar.

"Vanessa," he called out.

"In here."

Every time Kamal entered Vanessa's office he admired how the room seemed to almost vomit books upon him. They came from every conceivable angle. Had they been anything other than books, Vanessa might have been featured on that television show for hoarders, where workers would come in and shovel those books into piles and burn them at the end of the hall like Nazis at a bonfire.

"Have a seat." She pointed to the chair in front of her desk.

"I missed you yesterday," he said, half-joking.

"I was tied up—but I heard there was a low turnout at the bookstore."

She didn't have time to go to the signing, but she had time to follow up with the store, he mused. "Pretty small crowd. But you know how it is."

Vanessa nodded, but the expression on her face was clear: she had no idea "how it was."

Dispensing with the small talk, Vanessa began. "The publisher passed on your next novel. I went ahead and pitched it to a few others, and none of them were interested."

"But it's the best book I've written so far," Kamal said.

"Every author feels that way," Vanessa responded, shuffling papers on her desk. "The bottom line is these black nerd books are just not selling. I don't think publishers know how to market to black people beyond the urban market anyway, but that's besides the point. You're nowhere near recouping your advances, and the numbers just don't bear out for *anyone* to take on another book from you."

"There're people out there who buy books in my

genre," Kamal said. "Look at Junot Díaz, Mat Johnson, Victor LaValle, Percival Everett, Paul Beatty, and T. Geronimo Johnson," Kamal said, his mind flooding with the names of the authors he idolized. "Hell, every single one of Colson Whitehead's books is in a different genre. You can't tell me that there is no market for my voice."

"Well, Kamal, we can agree that you're not exactly a Colson Whitehead, can't we?"

"What do you mean?"

"You write like you have an MFA, but you don't."

"You're losing me," he said.

"A publisher wants to know how to deal with an author's books based on his or her pedigree."

"Damn," Kamal said, lowering his head. "If your opinion of me is so low, why did you even take me on as a client?"

"You were a gamble, and sadly the gamble just hasn't paid off."

"So what are you telling me? You're cutting me loose?"

Vanessa placed her manicured fingers in a steeple formation and rested them against her chin. "I just think you might have more success with a smaller press or even self-publishing. At this level, there's not a lot we can really do for each other going forward."

The anger burned in Kamal's chest for a moment before fizzling out into numbness. He knew things were bad, but he didn't realize they were *that* bad. In only a matter of minutes, he had discovered that both his publisher and his agent were ending their relationships with him. He wasn't even back to square one. He was worse off. Vanessa was right: no one would take him on with his poor sales history. In short, he was screwed.

"So that's it?" Kamal asked. "After all we've been through over these past few years, it ends like this?"

Vanessa lowered her hands to her desk and spread out her fingers patiently before her. "It's not personal. I still think of you as a friend, and as a friend, I can tell you that this is no longer the best route for your writing career. I'm just being honest."

"Brutally honest," he corrected. "This new book is a bestseller, and you know it. You don't want to pass on that, not after all of the work you've put into my career."

Vanessa smiled, almost facetiously. "I have read your book, and I can pretty safely say that it would be next to impossible for you to sell that book to any major publisher. Who's going to buy it? This book is even more left of center than your previous books—the ones that didn't sell. I think you might be overwriting to compensate for the fact that you don't have an MFA. Maybe you should take some time off to go and get one. Or you could go in the other direction and write something a bit more urban."

When the words left her mouth, Kamal immediately thought about Percival Everett's novel *Erasure*, a book that almost summed up his present existence to a tee. In the novel, a novelist—much like Kamal—decided to rebel against the publishing industry by writing an exaggerated take on the "urban novel," which ironically went on to become a bestseller. He would not allow himself to do that, though. He simply had too much pride to change stripes.

"All I can do is be me," he said, rising from his seat.

"I understand," Vanessa responded.

"So this is it?"

"Don't sound so final. One day our paths might cross again."

"But only if I change what I write about," Kamal said.

"The industry is small. If you decide to write something that *they* can sell, then we can talk about things again. In the meantime, I think you just need to focus on doing *you* for a while."

As Kamal descended the stairs, still incredulous to Vanessa's words, he felt a knot forming in his throat. No one said the publishing industry wasn't incredibly difficult for writers of color, but he hadn't realized how thoroughly Vanessa had bought into the status quo until just now.

As he stepped out of the building and onto the sidewalk, the overcast of the sky threatened to engulf him completely. He had no plan going forward. His dreams might as well have been dirt blowing along the street, the crumbs left from a city that was accustomed to devouring those who dared to dream.

## 4

When Kamal returned to his brownstone, he found Yasmin sitting on the steps out front, reading her recently signed copy of *A Junkyard of Absurdities*. The immediacy of her presence surprised him.

"Yasmin," Kamal said, approaching her. "What's up?"

She looked up casually, as if his finding her on the steps of his place was as natural as the hair on her head.

"I just wanted to stop by and see if you wanted to hang out—and since I didn't have your number—"

"But you clearly had my address."

"Hey, I didn't have anywhere to go."

"What are you talking about?"

"James came over, and I wanted to give him and Twan some privacy. I started out hitting up record stores downtown and getting some lunch, but then I figured I would see what you were up to."

Kamal liked that he was getting a chance to see Yasmin again, but he hated that Twan had basically nudged her out into a city she hardly knew. That was beyond tough love—but people do ridiculous things all the time when they're in love. Yasmin probably figured since James was over there that she could come over to Kamal's to hang out—like a roommate exchange. Today was just not the best day for him to be entertaining anyone, he thought. His world had just been shaken up, and he needed some time to lick his wounds. Still, he didn't like the idea of leaving Yasmin to sit out on the steps after she had been sitting there for who knows how long.

"Why don't you come up for a bit," Kamal said.

"You sure? I'm not trying to impose," she said. "I don't know if you have company coming by later or something."

"No one's coming by later. You can stay as long as you'd like."

---

"THIS IS A PRETTY BIG PLACE," YASMIN commented as she paced the main area of the apartment, which was just one wide open room that fed directly into the kitchen, the den area boxed off with a love seat and a couch.

"Yeah, it's all right." Kamal walked into the kitchen. "Want anything to drink?"

"Water—if you have it."

Kamal had to think for a second before he caught her joke. "Be thankful we have one of these water purifier knobs on our sink. Wouldn't want to toughen you up too much with the City water."

"I can take it. I can take anything this city throws at me." Yasmin was now in full laughter with jokes Kamal could barely comprehend.

In spite of himself, he smiled and that act alone lifted his spirits.

He returned to the couch with a glass of water and

handed it to her before sitting down. A forty-two inch LED television rested on the wall ahead of them, but neither moved for the remote control resting on the coffee table directly in front of them.

"Thank you," she said, taking the glass and placing it to her lips. "You look like you've had a pretty rough day. Wanna talk about it?"

When Kamal had first seen Yasmin on the steps of his brownstone, he vowed to himself that he would not spill his guts about what happened at Vanessa Travont's office, but now as he sat next to her, his back sinking into the fluffy, but worn, cushions of the couch, he could feel the pain and frustration wanting to leave his lips and fill the quiet void between them.

Registering his apprehension, Yasmin placed her glass on one of the coasters scattered across the table and took one of Kamal's hands into her own. "Come on. Spill it. Tell Mama what's wrong."

The smile on her face softened him a bit, and in that moment, seeing her eyes and taking them in for the first time (after all, she had worn shades most of that first day), he realized just how beautiful she was. Her smile was warm and tender, her face perfectly arranged in a way that should have made her beauty spectacularly obvious to him from the first moment he saw her. Instead, his view of the world had been jaded by the frustrations of his writing career. Now that his career was in complete free fall, he had nothing to lose by stepping outside of that bubble to experience what was directly in front of him.

*Wow*, he thought (and nearly said aloud) to himself. If he had been in his right mind, he would have been the one vying for *her* attention and time, but as fate would have it, she had come to him, although he suspected it to be more out of necessity than attraction.

He slowly parted his lips and began the story of how how he had been called to Vanessa Travont's office on a Sunday (of all days!) and how she had delivered the news of his being passed over by his publisher, while simultaneously dumping the horrendous news of her parting ways with him as his agent, all in the space of fifteen minutes. A weaker man might have walked over to her office window and leaped (the one floor) to the ground. It probably wouldn't have resulted in death, but a sprained ankle might have been symbolic in its own way.

When he finished, he closed his eyes and sighed heavily, leaning his head back onto the couch cushions. For a moment Yasmin said nothing, only stroked his hand softly.

"I could say a lot of cliche stuff right now, but I won't do that to you," she finally said. "What I *can* say to you, though, is this: you definitely have the talent to overcome this obstacle, regardless of what anyone else might tell you."

He didn't know why, but her words were more comforting that he had thought possible. He let each of those words drift over him like the gentle snowflakes of a surprise snowfall. In that moment he had the burning desire to lean over and kiss her, but he knew better than to put her in such a compromising position. If things went south, where exactly would she go? Back to Twan's place? At that moment he had only Twan and James to thank for their selfishness. If it were not for them, he might have at least confronted Yasmin with his interest in her. Instead, he took the thumb of the hand she was rubbing and rubbed her hand in return. In a way, the feeling of their hands rubbing each other was better than a kiss anyway.

## 5

In the days that followed, Kamal allowed himself to get lost in the feeling of getting to know Yasmin. He enjoyed her optimistic perspective on life, and in some ways she reminded him of the way he'd been when he first moved to The City, that time before the rawness of City life grated away his optimism.

Each day he allowed himself to reveal a little more of his growing interest in her, compliments, the multitude of things he genuinely admired about her. The only difference between then and now was that he no longer kept those things to himself.

Yasmin seemed to grow in the sunlight of his adoration, and it was only in her responses to his compliments that he became convinced she was just as interested in him as he was in her. Still, he had yet to make a move. He knew that if he were to take it beyond what it currently was, he would need to have some idea of what he wanted. It would be unfair of him to introduce a physically intimate component to their relationship just because he could. She didn't come across as a recreational woman—and that was one of the things that drew him even closer to her.

Another benefit of his growing romantic attraction to Yasmin was that it kept him from focusing on that giant abyss that was his writing career. His existence outside of writing revolved around two composition courses he taught as an adjunct and a part time gig as a temp over at a law firm, a job that consisted largely of him going out and investigating personal injury cases and taking pictures of the locations of car accidents and slip and falls. Occasionally, he was asked to serve lawsuits on people, a job he hated, as people tended to aim their ire at the messenger more often than not. His writing career had been the glue that made all of the other components of his work life bearable. In the absence of that, there was a void—and Yasmin was working wonders filling that void.

Did he actually *like* her or was she just a cushion from the harsh blow he had been dealt by Vanessa Travont? While he felt his feelings were genuine, he couldn't be absolutely sure. Instead, he hid behind hugs and warm smiles, anything to help him feel safe and connected.

"So have you decided what you're going to do with your latest novel, the one Vanessa gave back to you?" Yasmin asked, as they walked through City Park, an area that extended roughly forty blocks through the heart of the bustling metropolis.

The topic had ceased being taboo, so rather than begin his typical silent sulking about the worst day of his professional life, he answered matter-of-factly instead. "I'm thinking about sending it out to some smaller publishers maybe. I'm sure it's good enough to find a home somewhere."

"That's the right attitude to take," Yasmin offered. "Do you need any help in finding publishers? I saw this book at the bookstore the other day that had addresses for a lot of publishers. *Writers Market* or something like that."

"Sure," he said, willing to accept any help she could offer. "I appreciate it." He was aware of the writing books out there, but a major part of him had been spoiled when he got signed by a literary agent because that meant that he did not have to do that kind of research himself. The agent would open all of the doors that he himself could not open. He had fallen so fast, so quickly, that he had almost forgotten everything that Yasmin was now mentioning to him. "How is everything going with your job search?"

"It's coming along. I met with James's agent, Corky Simmons, and he said he would take me on and see about getting me some auditions set up."

"Wow! That's great news! Why are you just now telling me?" Kamal asked.

"I just didn't want to seem like I was rubbing it in your face—especially with all that you have been going through. Plus, I know auditions don't equal jobs, so I figured when I got my first job, I would tell you then."

"That cuts me deep, you know. I know I've been in a funk lately, but I'm really happy for you. I don't want you to worry about telling me great news because you're worried about my feelings. My feelings are small in the grand scheme of things. Your accomplishments are not. We should go celebrate somewhere!"

"How about we celebrate when I get an audition that goes well or something like that?" Yasmin responded.

"I can't believe what I'm hearing," he said. "You're the most optimistic person I know. Don't lose that about yourself. That's a beautiful trait to have—particularly in this city. Keep it and hold on to it for as long as you possibly can."

Yasmin smiled sheepishly.

"That's it. We're going to celebrate. Have you ever had one of the piña coladas from Emilio's Place?"

"No. Can't say I have."

"Emilio's is an institution in The City, and you haven't lived until you've had one of the Big Ass Coladas they serve over there. You up for a drink?"

"Sure. Why not?"

"Well, let's see if we can get over there before happy hour shuts down and we lose the half price special. Not trying to pinch pennies, but as you know, I'm one job short at this point," Kamal said, laughing.

Yasmin nudged him playfully and looped her arm through his as they stepped off the curb and hailed a taxi.

---

SHORTLY AFTER THEY ARRIVED AT EMILIO'S PLACE, Kamal ordered each of them a Big Ass Piña Colada, which was a gigantic glass of ice blended house mix infused with enough rum to spin Puerto Rico on its axis. The alcohol was camouflaged with a rich vanilla ice cream, the not-so-secret ingredient in Emilio's take on the piña colada. The average person would be doing well to finish one glass. Anyone who went beyond that clearly had an interest in getting much more than a buzz. If a person dared a third, then they probably needed to get professional help going forward.

The moment Yasmin took a sip of her drink, she put it down quickly and stared at the drink, raising it occasionally to admire it. "This is incredible!" she gushed.

"I know!" Kamal responded, taking a long, thick sip of the concoction. "You have to be careful though.

If you belched while smoking a cigarette, you might blow your face off your head."

Yasmin laughed, before diving into another sip, this one much longer. Even with a sip that lasted ten seconds, the drink line barely moved. That was the thing about Emilio's Big Ass Piña Coladas: by the time you saw the drink line move, you were already well on your way to being inebriated.

"Slow down. Seriously," Kamal said, taking another really long sip.

"Look who's talking!" she responded, laughing at him.

"I got stress in my life. That's my excuse," he responded.

For a moment, the two of them sipped from their drinks and giggled at little nothings that each of them muttered between sips. Finally, Kamal could feel his inhibitions lightening. He wanted to ask her questions he had not been able to bring himself to ask in his usual sober state.

"How are things working out for you over at Twan's?"

"It's a'ight. James damn-near lives over there. Every time I look up, I see him walking in and out of Twan's room or sitting in the kitchen munching on Funyuns. I can't complain, though. I'm just a guest, so I'm happy to just have a place to lay my head at night. Plus, the two of them are a trip! Finishing each other's sentences and all that. I feel like such a third wheel when I'm around them."

Kamal hadn't expected his question to elicit such a detailed response, but then the liquor was probably lubricating the conversation at this point.

"Well, if it gets too crowded over there, you are always welcome to spend the night at my place. I'm pretty sure James wouldn't mind, especially since he's always over at Twan's anyway."

"Kamal, you sound like you're proposing a roommate swap," Yasmin said playfully in a faux Cockney accent.

"Well, not exactly. Technically, a roommate swap would be if James stayed in the guest room you are using and you stayed in his room at my apartment. And, well, we know James is not sleeping in the guest room over there."

"So," she responded, slowly losing the accent, "are you proposing that I sleep in your room?"

It was such a sudden leap in the conversation, as if she had skipped over the steps in between, the buffer he was providing himself so that any suggestion of that nature be wrapped, beyond reproach, in a veil of logic.

"Hold on," he said quickly, taking another, extra long swig of his drink, while Yasmin waited patiently. "I don't want to make you feel uncomfortable around me."

"Okay," she responded, "but you are not answering my question, are you?"

"Well, would you want to sleep in my room?"

"You are being such a kid right now," Yasmin said. "Why do guys always try to act like they are all brand new when a woman brings up the topic of hooking up? Just be straight up with me. I can't be angry at your response, because I am the one asking the question. The least you can do is just be straight up with me."

"My bad," Kamal said, sitting his drink down. "Look. I know you're new to The City, and I know you haven't been here that long, but yes, I would definitely enjoy your company, should you want to come stay with me—in my room."

"See. Was that so hard?"

"That's what she said!" he joked.

"Oh, so you're one of *those* people," Yasmin said laughing.

"Do you want to spend the night with me?"

She took a long sip of her drink. "Not tonight. But it's nice to know that I have options now."

6

Around two o'clock in the morning the first wave of nausea hit. Kamal barely made it to the toilet bowl in time. After spilling nearly all of his dinner, he felt the dull ache in his stomach persisting. Rather than return to his bedroom, he sat down between the bathtub and the toilet bowl and pulled the waste basket close to him. He knew if the wave hit again, he wouldn't have enough time to go looking around, or even reaching around, for something to vomit into. Surely enough, within the next five minutes, he felt his stomach involuntarily contract, and what remained in his stomach came projecting from his mouth in one long, uncontrolled stream—and then another. As he groaned in fatigue while trying to collect himself, he silently thanked Yasmin for not agreeing to come over and stay the night. He would have hated to have her witness him like this: body hugging the porcelain throne tightly, with that cool, smooth bowl pressed tightly against his cheek. There was not much comfort he could get from his present state, but the coolness of the toilet bowl was the closest thing to a reprieve available.

He threw up twice more before resigning himself

to the fact that he was actually done throwing up. It was now after three thirty, and his alarm had already been set to go off in three hours so that he could make it to the law office by eight that morning. For a moment he considered calling in sick, but that was not a luxury that he had as a temporary employee. If they decided to take him on, he would not only get sick days, but he would get vacation days, too. While he knew that was a road he should have been angling himself on to, he had always viewed work—of any kind—as something to pay the bills while he wrote his novels. And he had only planned to do that until he had accumulated a strong enough backlist that he could carve out a living writing books full-time.

Lying there, hugged against the toilet, though, he realized that his future as a writer was precarious, at best. He had no plan beyond what he and Yasmin had discussed, so he vowed to go by the bookstore during his lunch break and pick up the book she had mentioned and begin the process of submitting work to some of the smaller publishing houses that didn't require literary agents to be a part of the equation.

Surely he could bounce back. He believed in himself enough to not give up, and he believed that the novel he had written deserved to be published. There was a publisher out there waiting for a manuscript like his, he reasoned, and as he tried to sleep the few remaining hours before his alarm went off, he tried to force himself to dream of the plethora of options that would be awaiting him.

---

KAMAL FUMBLED THROUGH THE DAY, COMPETENT enough to do his job, but not much else. Over his lunch break, he picked up the *Writer's Market* book Yasmin had suggested. Later that evening, shortly after Yasmin came by to visit, the two of them, armed with highlighters, ink pens, and notebooks, proceeded to comb through the entire volume, listing the types of independent publishers that might be interested in his novel.

"What exactly is your book about?" Yasmin asked, lying on her stomach, her chin resting in the palm of one of her hands.

"This one is about a farmer who is a widower and how he struggles to raise his daughter after the death of his wife. It's set in Mississippi, just outside of a town like the one I grew up in."

Yasmin nodded her head. "Well, that's different from what you've written about in the past."

"Yeah, I know. It doesn't exactly smack of what you would find on the urban table at Barnes & Noble," he said.

"Definitely not."

"If I didn't know that you had written a story like that, I might have thought it was written by some white guy. After all, they're the ones who write those kinds of stories."

"That's what would have made the book so special. It would've shown another slice of Southern African-American life, something that's not usually included in the 21st century portion of the literary canon," Kamal said. "I know." He paused. "I take my writing way too seriously. I mean, who talks about his work in relationship to the larger literary canon. Too much ego, I guess."

Yasmin responded, "To be creative, you have to have an ego. I mean, look at me. I actually got on a plane and flew up here because I had the audacity to think my voice was special enough for me to make a living using it. Every morning when I wake up and go to an audition, knowing the possibility of getting a call-back is slim, I have to believe I am better than good. So don't look at that as a negative trait. Visualize it and plan accordingly."

"Okay, Oprah Jr.," he joked.

Once they had completed their list, they looked at it and double-checked to see if the publisher was actually seeking that kind of work. Once they had done that, they searched out the publishers who accepted online queries or submissions. There was no point in buying postage and making a lot of physical copies if he did not have to. By the time they finished, they had gotten the list down to thirty-two names.

"Your new publishing home is in this list," Yasmin proclaimed.

"From your mouth to the universe's ears," Kamal said.

"So you know what you have to do now."

"Yep."

Yasmin yawned and covered her mouth.

"You're welcome to stay here," Kamal offered.

"I don't know. I should probably go ahead and leave while I'm still awake. I can get a cab."

"Yasmin, you don't have to do all that. Just stay the night. You can have my room. I'll sleep on the couch. I just don't want you out there late at night in The City. Come on. Just stay. I promise I won't try anything."

She yawned again. "I don't have my stuff with me."

"I have an extra toothbrush in the medicine cabinet. Anything else you need I can pick up from the corner bodega."

"Are you sure about me staying?"

"I'm positive."

"Thank you," she said, rising to her feet and stretching.

Kamal showed her to his room and got her settled in, before returning to the couch with a blanket and passing out as soon as his head kissed the cushions.

## 7

Adrenaline propelled Kamal through the rest of the week, as he sent out email after email after email, in hopes of finding a new home for his third novel. He had finally given it a name: *The Princess of Fall,* a title that referenced the opening scene, in which the protagonist's daughter dances in a crude ballet style through the rows of corn in the field adjacent to their home. The title was just something to give an official air to the project. If a publisher wanted to change it to something more marketable, Kamal had no problem with that.

Once he reached the thirty-second name on the list, he silently applauded himself for taking such a huge step without Vanessa Travont. Now, the only thing left for him to do was to begin the unavoidable process of waiting to hear back from the publishing houses that would actually respond.

While this step in the process was torturous, since it didn't have a clear ending in sight, Kamal reminded himself that he had done his part by taking the step of putting his work out into the universe for others to either accept or reject.

For the moment he was still an author shopping a

book, and the feeling of not being helpless in the way he had been after that fiasco with Vanessa Travont was especially motivational to him.

Maybe Yasmin was right and he would find a new publishing home from that list. He hoped that she was. He could feel the self-doubt bubbling beneath his confidence, and the only thing he knew that would keep that feeling at bay was to receive an acceptance from one of the companies—any of the companies, actually.

Kamal sent the last email with a flourish of his wrist. He smiled and closed his laptop.

JAMES THOMAS OFTEN WALKED AROUND BARELY emitting a sound. Having marched in military-style marching bands in junior high, high school, and college, he tended to roll his feet softly as he walked, which had the odd effect of stabilizing his six foot three inch, one hundred ninety pound, muscular frame in an almost *too* perfect alignment. He looked as if, at any moment, he could pirouette and break out a rond de jambe move, or, on the contrary, catch the game winning sixty yard pass from a quarterback during the final seconds of the championship game. But James preferred playing the snare drum, where he was first chair for four years of high school and four years of college. He had never even attempted to sing publicly until his junior year of college, and once he had been bitten by the "musical bug," he threw himself completely into it. Within two years of graduating from college, he would have an ensemble part in a major musical in The City, with prospects galore going forward.

Kamal had learned all of this from James during the first two weeks of their living together, yet he still managed to get the bejeezus shocked out of him when he would look up, after assuming he was alone in the den, and see James float casually into his peripheral vision with the quietness of a mouse pissing on a soft patch of cotton. He did not know if he would ever get used to a guy that big moving like a ninja across the floor. It took James coming out of his room for Kamal to even know he had come home.

"Hey, Kamal," James said, strolling across the kitchen floor. "I hear you have a new friend."

Kamal chuckled. "Was that your plan? You and Twan wanted to put us together?"

"I don't know what you're talking about," James said, smiling. "You know me. I am *not* a match maker."

"Yeah, right," Kamal responded. "Is that your final answer or are you going to at least give me the respect of telling me what you guys were thinking?"

"Before I say anything that might incriminate me, I have to ask you this one question: do you like her? I mean, isn't she great?"

"That's two questions, and I guess it's safe to say the answer to both of those questions is yes."

"I knew it! When Twan first told me about her and showed me a picture, I knew that you two would hit it off."

Kamal walked over to the refrigerator, took out a bowl of fruit, and walked over to the kitchen table to sit down. "You know, if you guys wanted us to connect in a more traditional way, we could have at least done a double date or something. Instead, you guys basically kick her out of Twan's place and force her to come over here."

"Is that what she told you?" James asked, his smile unable to conceal his animated incredulity.

"Yeah, isn't that what happened?"

"I guess so."

"No, seriously. What happened?"

James sat down at the table across from Kamal and reached for a few grapes from Kamal's bowl. "If she said that's what happened and everything is working out for the two of you, then who am I to contradict that?"

Kamal hated when James played games like this. It was almost as if James thought ignorance was always blissful when people seemed happy already. Living with him for going on three years, Kamal had yet to change his assessment of his roommate when it came to that issue.

"So am I going to have to bribe you to get a straight answer out of you?" Kamal asked, joking.

"Naw, I'll give you the 411 for free—this time," James said, laughing. "Did she tell you that she was a fan of your work when she met you?"

"Yeah. What? That wasn't true?"

"It was definitely true. She had already planned to come to The City and stay with Twan for a while, but when she found out by accident that you and I were roommates, she pleaded with him to introduce her to you. After the book signing over at Nell's, she was completely smitten with you. She could not stop talking about you, but she didn't think that you appeared that interested in her. Twan tried to tell her that you were just under some stress as of late, but I don't think that she bought that. Dude, I can't begin to tell you how much she interrogated me about you. Finally, Twan and I just told her that she had to get out of the apartment. She could either bust a move and tell you how she felt or she could stop talking our ears off about you. I think that's when she came over here. And, well, the rest is history. The good thing, though, is that she doesn't talk our ears off any more, so I guess you guys are doing all of the talking to each other."

Kamal reached for an apple out of the bowl and bit down into it. So that was her plan, he thought. He had been completely obtuse when it came to what was going on around him. Three people were apparently working together—conspiring together—to make this happen. While the idea of it all made him feel a bit uneasy, he thought about it for a moment and realized that he would have probably conspired in a similar way to initiate contact with her if his head had been much clearer.

"I still can't believe she had all of that to say about me," Kamal finally said. "I would have probably have busted a move in my own time."

"I know," James said, smiling, "but I know that you've been a bit down about your writing life, and I figured it wouldn't hurt too much to let the situation play out with her approaching you. It was all her idea anyway. And, not trying to get all in your Kool-Aid, but you haven't been going out much in the past year. I'm not saying that JoAnna didn't do you foul, but I didn't expect for you to draw into a shell and not date anyone else. You needed this attention from Yasmin. Dude, you look like you're blossoming into your old self again."

James was the only person who could have put Kamal's past back in his face so effortlessly, without any ill intent. It was impossible for Kamal to feel a way about that, either. In many ways, James was one of his best friends, which is why they had managed to room together for three years without any problems.

He knew Twan and James wanted him to be happy, and when Kamal considered how Twan had thought enough of him to be cool with him dating Yasmin, he knew he did not want to take any of this budding good fortune for granted.

"So when are you guys connecting again?" James asked.

"We're getting a bite to eat later this evening."

"That's cool. I'll be over at Twan's so that you two can have some privacy."

"Is that why you've been spending so much time over there lately?" Kamal asked. Typically, James stayed with Twan a few days a week, nothing like the overtime he had been pulling in recent days.

"Hey," James responded, barely concealing his smile. "I don't know what you're talking about."

He stood up and grabbed a few more grapes from Kamal's bowl before doing an about face and rolling his feet back into his bedroom, closing the door behind himself.

Kamal had a fleeting thought of an episode of *A Different World*, where everyone was trying to help Kimberly Reese pay for her college tuition. Mr. Gaines had said, "People have to sneak around behind your back trying to help you." Out of the four of them, Kamal was finally aware of what was going on, and that gave him a sense of comfort that he was moving in the right direction for the first time in quite a while.

8

Kamal had not expected the first few rejections of his novel to come back so quickly. Within three weeks, he received three rejections. He had expected to wait closer to six months to hear back from anyone. Did they have people lined up, waiting to send the rejection letters out the day they received the query? So this was what it was like getting rejected from the slush pile by an intern, Kamal figured. To add further fuel to his frustrations, he missed Yasmin, who had spent the last week doing a string of auditions Corky Simmons set up for her that left her without any time to hang out. They had, however, kept in touch over the phone.

In all of the weeks they had been hanging out, they still had yet to move beyond doing anything platonic. For the life of him, Kamal could not figure out what was going on. He thought that she liked him as much as he liked her, but it seemed as if she was pulling back a little bit from him. Did she know that James had told her about their plan? Whatever was going on was confusing him at this point—yet it all made him want her more, so maybe that was the point of it all.

Outside of the empty hours in his evening and the

quicksand feeling of being sucked down into the end-less of abyss of failure as a writer, he contemplated what his life would be like if he completely threw him-self into his remaining two jobs. Maybe he should con-sider going to law school. That was what a number of his classmates from Ellison-Wright College had done after graduating. He could function in an environment ensconced in books and writing. The three years of law school would be like an incubation period where he could grow to accept himself as being something other than a novelist. Who knew? Maybe the law firm he presently temped for might consider hiring him as an associate one day. That might effectively take care of his financial irritations, too. At present, it took all three of his gigs to come up with rent and food. If he were a lawyer in The City, he would need to only have that one job, and he would likely make much more than he could have with any combination of smaller part-time jobs.

Still, Kamal could not shake the idea that he wanted to write. Being a writer was not just something you picked up and put down. It had never been a lu-crative profession for most practitioners who engaged in it, but the love of putting the pen to the page often overcame the shortfalls of small advances and even smaller royalty checks. Of course, if Kamal wrote a bestseller and that bestseller was made into a successful movie, then he could possibly make more writing than he could practicing law. It was a bit like winning the lottery, he acknowledged to himself, but at the same time, you could never win the lottery if you never played it.

When he thought about the rejection that had been mounting since he had become a professional writer, he could feel the swell of self-pity taking over him. He knew in his heart that he worked too hard to get to this point in his career to just start over from scratch. He even allowed himself to consider this for a moment: if he actually did start over, what would he do differently that he did not do the first time? He wracked his brain long and hard and nothing came to mind.

Then something Yasmin said to him earlier resurfaced: "If I didn't know that you had written a story like that, I might have thought it was written by some white guy. After all, they are the ones who write those kinds of stories and get them published."

The fine hairs on the back of Kamal's neck stood up. The idea seemed almost too silly to even consider, yet it was too irresistible to disregard. Could he actually edit the manuscript and market it as a white author? People had been using pseudonyms to conceal gender and ethnicity for quite some time, yet the idea had never crossed Kamal's mind.

He vowed to do a little research before making a decision. After all, he wanted to make sure that if he went down that road, he had a viable plan.

———

REJECTIONS CONTINUED TO DRIFT IN AS KAMAL did his research on the publishing industry. He combed websites, trade periodicals, blogs, and podcasts, all the time wondering to himself why he had not investigated any of this much earlier. After all, writing was his chosen vocation. To have come this far with his career and still be oblivious to how race impacts books sales, he wanted to kick himself for his willful ignorance.

Early in his research, he scanned the *New York*

*Times* bestseller lists from the past five years and then went on to check the rankings on Amazon, not by specific genre category, but by general fiction standards. He poured over lists and rankings of African-American authors and compared them to lists that included white authors. When it came to books that were non-urban in nature, he noticed a curious thing: there were not many people of color on the list, and the people of color that were listed were not African-American. There were several African writers, mainly from Nigeria; several bi-racial writers from England; and a smattering of writers from the Caribbean Islands. The diaspora was represented in small, peculiar numbers, but those numbers included very few African Americans. It was as if the larger white publishing establishment had grown bored with African-American writers after Toni Morrison won her Nobel Prize for Literature in 1993. Of course there were outliers, like Walter Mosley, Terri McMillan, and Eric Jerome Dickey, but there were hardly any beginner or debut novelists of great acclaim who were African-American. There were no equivalents to Stephen King, John Grisham, Danielle Steele, J.K. Rowling, Dan Brown, or Neil Gaiman. There were just the urban-centric authors and the non-urban centric authors, this disparate group that often shared the same table at the chain bookstores. J. California Cooper and K'wan side by side, just as Mother Nature intended.

Kamal realized that the odds of even a white writer making a great living from writing novels was a remote possibility. Still, there were white authors he could point to who were doing it on the biggest of levels, whereas there were no African-American authors he could point to *at all* who were killing it across the board, consistently.

Another thing he noticed was that the subject matter range of white authors was unlimited. They could write anything they wanted, without regard to how it would be positioned ethnically. White authors could write awesome books about time travel or the future of the Internet. They could write books about Jewish angst and mother issues and masturbation. They could even write books about race to unburden themselves of racial guilt and white privilege. What could African-American novelists write about? Thugs and baby mamas, slavery, civil rights, and modern (or futuristic) takes on any of those things. Of course, he believed in his heart that African Americans were far more diverse than the publishing industry was willing to believe—at least as a business model—but it just seemed that those were the themes and archetypical tropes that they felt most comfortable and capable of marketing.

No amount of hash tagging on Twitter was going to change that fact any time soon, especially within the largest of the publishing companies. It was a wonder any of Kamal's books had even been published in the first place. Stallings Press was bucking the system, and he guessed the numbers just did not bear out for them to continue their little experiment.

He also couldn't fault Vanessa Travont for being able to read the tea leaves far better than he. She was a literary agent, and she earned her commission off of her ability to sell books to major publishers, books those publishers could then actually sell to consumers using their existing business models. It made little sense for her to take on a book she knew would not fit that mold. She would have been better off acquiring clients whose books she knew she could sell in the current publishing climate. Of course she could have been a bit more diplomatic about how things went down, but that was neither here nor there.

The whole exercise in researching diversity in publishing depressed Kamal, and he considered just giving up writing altogether and seeing if he had it in him to do something else creative. The problem was that he only knew how to write. That was his talent, his special skill. He could probably do other things, but not as well as he could write.

On the verge of frustrated tears, he opened the folder on his laptop that contained *The Princess of Fall*. He printed out the full manuscript and grabbed a red pen.

Since no one seemed to think his novel was *black* enough, he decided to take a chance and see exactly how *white* it was.

9

Kamal's cell phone awakened him with its persistent vibrating. He sat up, unaware he had fallen asleep with his face pressed against the pages of his manuscript. Answering the phone, he yawned, positioning the phone as far away from his mouth as possible.

"Hello," he managed.

"Were you sleeping?" Yasmin asked.

"I just dozed off for a minute. Why? What's up?"

"It's only eight o'clock in the evening."

"Oh. I had no idea," he said, wiping the dried saliva from the side of his mouth.

"Are you up for company tonight?" Yasmin asked.

"Yes," he said, almost too enthusiastically, as he hopped up from his desk and headed for the bathroom to brush his teeth.

"Well, I can be over there in an hour, if that's cool."

"Sounds good," Kamal said, excited that he was finally getting to spend time with her. "Was there anything you wanted to go out and do tonight?"

"I just want to stay in a kick it with you," she responded. "Do you have Netflix?"

"Nope, but I can have it turned on before you get over here."

"I'm just joking. You know 'Netflix and Chill.'" She laughed at her own joke.

*Was she suggesting what he thought she was suggesting?* He prayed that she was.

"Well, I'll see you soon," she said, before hanging up.

Kamal put the phone down and brushed his teeth thoroughly, then gargled with spearmint mouthwash. He jumped in the shower and scrubbed himself down. When he finished, he tossed on one of his black v-neck t-shirts and a pair of dark blue jeans. He straightened his room and lit a few candles around the apartment to kill any funky scents that he had grown too familiar with to recognize, unless he was entering the apartment after having been gone for a while. He even put on one of his most recent musical acquisitions, The Internet's *Ego Death,* and piped it through the Bluetooth speakers strategically placed throughout the room.

Going back to his desk, he put his manuscript into two neat stacks: the part that he had already begun to edit and the part he had yet to touch. He turned off the desk lamp and pulled the roll top portion of his desk down to cover up his work.

From there, he went into the den, sat down on the couch, and closed his eyes, excited and nervous at the thought of embracing Yasmin.

---

Yasmin was punctual, almost to the exact minute, and Kamal leapt to his feet as soon as he heard the soft rapping against the door. He opened the door, half-expecting to see her standing there in a trench coat tied at the waist and a pair of pumps, *Boomerang* style. Even though the movie was a throwback to the nineties, he still harbored fantasies of a woman making that scene come true in his real life. When he opened the door and saw Yasmin standing there in short shorts, a cut-up *Purple Rain* t-shirt, a funky purple fedora, and her hair braided and pulled into a bun in the back, Kamal almost did a backflip. It wasn't *Boomerang*, but it was the sexy Afro Punk chic that he loved about her style already, amped to the tenth power. He reached for her instinctively, and she reveled in his embrace, moaning her approval, as if his hug were the only thing in her life that had been missing until that moment.

"Damn, I missed you so much," he said softly, his breath punctuating the side of her neck. And then, just like that, he planted a kiss there.

She reached around his shoulders and pulled him closer, and his tongue eagerly found its way to the nape of her neck. She moaned again before stepping back away from him and collecting herself.

"Wow. Quite a welcome right there."

"I'm sorry. I couldn't help myself."

"I'm not complaining," Yasmin said, pushing her index finger softly into his chest and dragging it down his pecs slowly. Then she noticed the room, the music, and the mood. She stepped away from him and walked around slowly, taking in the change, a smile perched upon her lips. "All this for me?"

"Well, I know we haven't seen each other in over a week, and I just wanted to make sure the place didn't look like a straight-up man cave in here."

She chuckled. "Can I use your bathroom?"

"Sure," he said, pointing her to the bathroom situated directly between his room and James's room.

"I'll be right back."

Kamal tried not to study the sweet, sway of her body as she walked past him and into the bathroom, but he found it nearly impossible to ignore. Only when she closed the door behind herself did he look away. The music playing in the background suddenly rose into his focus, and he wondered if the crooning of Syd tha Kid was too much, too soon, for Yasmin. He doubted that it was. After all, they had been playing this game of cat and mouse for a while now, and he was well beyond pretenses at this point.

He walked over to the couch and sat down, facing the dark flatscreen television. He debated turning it on, but decided against it, choosing instead to close his eyes for moment and let the music wash over him in waves.

He could hear the bathroom door opening behind him, but he did not turn his head. Within seconds he could feel Yasmin's hands reaching around his head and softly pressing against his eyelids. She leaned down close to his right ear, her breath tickling him. "Do you still want me?"

The words were the invitation he had been seeking for weeks, but before he could respond to her question, he could feel the softness of her tongue, like a feather, brush against the outer edge of his ear.

He slowly lifted his face to meet hers, and their lips met, briefly at first, as they allowed that newness of their flesh pressed against the other to settle over them. When their tongues engaged, Kamal pulled her onto him, and they disappeared within the strings of the music blanketing the room.

In the middle of the night, Kamal woke to Yasmin's nude body pressed tightly against his, like a comforter shielding her from the air whipping about by the low level ceiling fan above their bodies. He kissed her forehead softly, and she responded by easing a hand up and down his chest. Their lips met again, and she slowly climbed atop him, blurring the line between the most delicious of dreams and the real, living, breathing art born of pure ecstasy.

## 10

S hakespeare had once written that "a rose by any other name would smell as sweet" in his play *Romeo and Juliet*, but Kamal had serious misgivings about that phrase when applied to the larger companies in the publishing industry. The industry had shown time and time again that it mattered what name was attached to a novel for it to sell—and not just in the sense of avoiding having a horror novelist with a name like Frankie Lifshitz. There was a legion of women writers working with male names, or, at minimum, using initials from their first and middle names to shift the focus from their names to the actual content of their books. There were also a myriad of articles where authors had demonstrated, quantitatively, that they got greater responses off of the exact same work just by changing the name attached to the work, whether it be a white woman using a white man's name or a white man using and Asian man's name. That rose was clearly sweeter when given another name.

Then there was the cover issue, Kamal noticed. African-American titles, urban and otherwise, tended to have pictures of African Americans front and center. Using people on the covers of books was common practice across the board, regardless of ethnicity, but there were not many African-American titles that did not include people. It was almost as if the publishers believed that African Americans would not buy books by other African Americans if there was no one on the cover who looked like them. As a result, even books that were not urban in nature still gave off an urban vibe. It was almost as if some publishers were saying, "Hey, black people! Here is the kind of book you like. See the cover? The one that looks like a nineties rap album? Yeah, that one. That's your book right there." Kamal imagined that African readers might have had the same frustration with seeing book covers of that sole baobab tree with a huge setting sun behind it. That was what Africa (the entire continent) looked like, right? A single tree with a piercing sun behind it. Any book cover that did not fit that stylistic structure looked wildly out of place when placed on a table alongside the others. It was almost like that song Kamal found himself unable to forget from his childhood, "One of These Things Is Not Like the Other."

As he pondered what name to use, he thought about his own name. His father, who passed away from cancer when Kamal was three, had named him after his favorite emcee, Q-Tip, one of the key members (as well as the co-founder) of the legendary rap group A Tribe Called Quest. Q-Tip was born Jonathan Davis, but he changed his name to Kamaal Ibn John Fareed when he converted to Islam. Kamal's father decided to go with Kamal, as opposed to Jonathan, and inadvertently left the third "a" in the name off the birth certificate, thereby resigning Kamal to a childhood of people calling him "camel" and making lame jokes and puns that played off that word.

Then there was the surname Jackson, a name that,

in spite of being connected to a U.S. President, often evoked the idea of blackness in most people. Kamal often had people crack jokes on his name as being the kind of name that wreaked of the greasiest fried chicken and largest, most swollen cuts of watermelon. The only two things that spared Kamal from the persistent verbal abuse of his classmates was (1) the fact that he shared a surname with the legendary entertainer Michael Jackson, and (2) his name was not Jenkins.

Writing the kind of novels that he wrote with a name that clearly connoted his ethnicity, he fell into an odd space in the publishing paradigm. Whatever name he came up with going forward, though, had to deflect that type of stereotyping and open the door to people reading the work before passing judgment on him as an author.

He decided to comb through baby names on the Internet, and when nothing jumped out at him, he took to recording street names in his notebook and jotting down names that he heard on television, even going as far as recording certain names that played in the credits of movies. Still, he was undecided. There was a part of him that considered the possibility that he was selling out, and that part of him stunted his ability to be conclusive in any decisions factoring into his plan. As a result, he kept all of his wild ideas to himself, unsure if he should reveal his plan to anyone, including Yasmin.

In the meantime, he continued editing his manuscript privately, already having given up hope that any of the remaining publishers from the list of thirty-two would accept the book for publication. His rejections were pre-ordained, no different from his need to go down swinging, regardless of which way the winds of fate blew.

"I got a job singing!" Yasmin yelled, embracing Kamal tightly. They were standing just inside the threshold of his apartment, the door still ajar.

"That's wonderful!" he said, lifting her from the ground and swinging her in a circle. When he placed her down, he pushed the door closed with his foot. "So tell me about it."

She reached for his hand and pulled him into his bedroom, where she sat down on the bed and leaned back on her elbows. "It's a small gig, but it's a gig nonetheless. There's a real check attached to it!"

"What is it?" Kamal asked again, happy for her, but nudging her to complete her thought.

"I will be singing in a house band at Louie's Jazz Lounge downtown. And guess what? I got it on my own. I just answered an ad in the weekly circular and went to the audition."

"That's great news!" Kamal said, kneeling down in front of her and kissing each of her hands, one at a time. "What about Corky Simmons?"

"He's still setting up auditions for me. The way I see it, I can do the Louie gig on Friday and Saturday evenings, and that would still give me time to make my rounds."

"So if you got a job—a play, say— that forced you to work on Friday night and Saturday nights, then you would give up this gig?"

Yasmin shrugged, still riding the wave of bliss. "I will cross that bridge when I come to it. You have to admit it, though. That's actually a wonderful problem to have for a person who has been eating through her savings since she got into town."

"Hey, I feel you. And I'm so happy for you!" Kamal leaned over and kissed her tenderly on the lips. "I guess we should be celebrating tonight then."

"If it's okay with you, I'd just like to stay in tonight."

"Sure. We can stream a movie or something and send out for pizza or Chinese food."

"I have a better idea," Yasmin said, smiling. "Have you ever heard *Maxwell's Urban Hang Suite?*"

"No. What's that?"

"You know the singer Maxwell, right? Well, that's his first album. It's a concept album where all of the songs work together to tell a single story. It's really dope. Kind of like a nineties version of Marvin Gaye's *I Want You.*"

"All right," Kamal said, the intonation in his voice lifting a bit, as if to suggest, "How does this factor into what you want to do?"

"Well, I want us to listen to the entire album together."

That was definitely a first, Kamal thought. He had listened to songs with women before, but not to the point of doing a private listening party for the entire album. Still, it was Yasmin's night to celebrate, and if that was the way she wanted to spend it, them listening to an old school album all night, then he was more than willing to comply.

"Cool," he responded.

"Here is the thing though: I want you to make love to me throughout the course of the entire album, from the first beat of the first song to the final fade out of the last one."

"Hey, no problem!" Kamal responded, clearly ready to accept the challenge. "I wouldn't have it any other way."

"Good," Yasmin said, lifting her shirt up. "But just keep in mind that the last track on the album is about thirteen minutes, with about six minutes of silence built into it."

"Wow. Interesting."

"Yeah," she said. "Maxwell said he wanted people to be able to hear themselves making love during the song. I wonder what we will sound like when we reach the final song."

Kamal helped her lift her shirt over her head. "I have no idea, but trust me; I am just as eager as you are to find out."

---

IN THE MIDDLE OF THE NIGHT KAMAL AWOKE AND immediately reached for Yasmin, his body fully rejuvenated and ready for another round, in spite of his general fatigue and sleepiness. His arm swept back and forth across her side of the bed, and when he did not feel her body, he immediately opened his eyes and sat up in bed, his eyes drawn to the lamp on his roll top desk with the lid open, just as he had accidentally left it. That is when he noticed that Yasmin was deep into reading his manuscript, at least two-thirds of the pages already turned face down, clearly read.

"Hey, Yaz," he said, calling her by her nickname for the first time since they had met. "You over there reading my book, I see." At first he thought he would be bothered by her snooping around in his things, but he quickly realized that she was not exactly snooping around. He had left the desktop up, so the manuscript was sitting out there for anyone to see. He could not be upset that she was reading it, especially since she enjoyed his writing so much.

"I couldn't sleep."

"Was I snoring too loudly?" Kamal asked.

"No. I just get restless at night sometimes. I got up and went to the bathroom, and when I saw your book sitting there, I couldn't resist the urge to read it."

He wanted so badly to ask her what she thought of it, but he didn't want to come across as too eager, so he simply responded, "Cool."

Yasmin turned the page she had just finished reading down onto the stack of read pages. She then stopped and looked up. "Can I ask you a question?" she said.

"Sure. What's up?"

"At first I thought I was looking at a manuscript with basic editing going on. I saw red lines striking through things and notes in the margin, and I was like, okay, I get it. But after a while I started to notice a few things and that made me go back and look at the other changes you made."

"So what's your question?" Kamal asked.

"Are you trying to scrub away any traces of the fact that you're a black writer?"

"Why do you say that?" Kamal asked, feigning both ignorant and blasé.

"My gut is telling me that you are writing this book and aiming it at a white audience. Is that what you're trying to do?"

"What are you talking about?"

"Kamal, don't play dumb with me. You know exactly what I'm talking about. I have read every book you've written, and while they're not dripping with ethnic signifiers, there was still this authentic voice that reflected who you were as a black man. But this book seems to have all of those things I love about your writing scratched out and replaced with these vanilla descriptions and plain dialogue. I know I am not a writer, but I read a lot and I know the styles of the authors I enjoy reading. Just tell me. You're whitewashing this book, aren't you?"

Kamal took a deep breath and ran his hands over his face to wake himself. He did not mind that she had discovered the manuscript. He did not even mind that she had put two and two together on what he was trying to accomplish with the manuscript, either. What he did care about, however, was the accusatory tone in her voice. It was as if she was passing a judgment on what he was doing. She wouldn't understand, he thought, and he didn't want to have an unnecessary argument with her because of that.

"I am just experimenting with the manuscript to see how it might read if I softened a few things, you know. Made it more universally palatable." It was euphemistic, and, yes, it was total bullshit.

"As an artist, your voice is all you have, and people have to take it or leave it, but we can't compromise our vision just to make ourselves more 'palatable.'"

Kamal nodded his head, wanting to take her comments in stride, but he couldn't resist asking her about her own job, the one they had just been celebrating a few hours earlier. "Will you be singing any songs that *you* wrote at your new job at Louie's?"

"No. But what does that have to do with anything?"

"You will be performing covers, which means that you will be tailoring your singing to fit what that audience wants and expects out of you. How is that any different than what I am doing?"

Yasmin sighed, shaking her head back and forth slowly. "You don't get it. I sing songs that last a few minutes. I'm like a real live juke box right now. That is not my goal! That is not where I want to be in a few years! You really just don't get it. You are a novelist. People spend hours inside of your imagination, that unique and beautiful imagination of yours. What I would not give to have people do that one day with my own songs! You are already there, in spades, and you want to compare yourself to me, a girl just starting out in the business? Wow. That is so not what I expected of you."

Kamal lay back on his bed, frustrated. "I don't want to argue with you. We were having a beautiful evening and then you start shitting all over my book."

Yasmin stood up and walked over to him, her beautiful nude form muted by the words still hanging in the air. "I'm sorry," she said, crawling up next to him. She placed a hand between his legs and began massaging him. "Do you forgive me?" she said, coyly. "*He* forgives me," she added, acknowledging his growing erection.

He sighed, conceding that maybe he had been a little bit too sensitive. "Yes. I'm sorry. I'm just tripping," he said, pulling her body against his.

She kissed him deeply, before looking into his eyes, the lamp illuminating the halo of her hair. "And just so you know. I was not *shitting* on your book. I was just letting you know that I really like the part that is beneath the red markings. That's all."

## 12

# 6 MONTHS LATER

The routine around the apartment had become comfortably and happily predictable. James continued to room with Kamal, but he still spent a great portion of the week at Twan's place; meanwhile, Yasmin spent the night several times a week with Kamal, although technically she was now paying rent at Twan's place. The system the four of them had worked out benefited everyone. James, while totally in love with Twan, still craved space, as did Twan, so their keeping separate places served to strengthen the quality of the time they spent together. Yasmin benefited in the sense that she was paying a much lower rent, mainly because she was volunteering to pay what she could afford to a cousin who was not pressed for anything at all, thanks to several lucrative contracts as a stylist for certain celebrities. Twan understood Yasmin's desire to contribute and did not deny her the opportunity to feel like she was carrying her own weight. Kamal, however, was probably the most fortunate of all three, though. Nothing changed as far as he was concerned—at least in the financial sense. If Yasmin had moved into his apartment and James had moved out, he would likely be expected to pay the full amount by himself, he suspected, and his meager paychecks did not extend far enough for that. Of course, there was always his writing which could bring in any unknown amount of money one day, although it had yet to bear any fruit.

Since the night he and Yasmin shared their "urban hang suite," he had quietly abandoned his novel, choosing to let the acceptance or rejection scenarios play out with the remaining publishers to whom he had submitted the original, unchanged version. In the meantime, he had begun doing research on self-publishing his work and concluded the best way to test the waters was with a novella he had been working on. His rationale for starting with a novella was built around the premise that, of the three major lengths of fiction out there (short stories, novellas, and novels), the novella was by far the least marketable to publishers. A writer could always submit short stories to an anthology or literary journal. A writer could also submit full-length novels to literary agents and publishers, big and small. But with novellas, the anthology editors and literary journals did not know what to do with them, for the most part, and publishers viewed them largely as not cost efficient. They did not sell as well as novels and often times cost just as much to produce. The only way to make a novella attractive to most publishers was to cobble together a novella with several short stories, and in the current publishing climate, few publishers found short story collections lucrative, even the ones written by big name writers. For a writer of Kamal's status, a publisher, major or independent, would never take that risk.

If no one would want to publish his novella, it left only one option: he would have to publish it himself. At first he found the idea unappealing, mainly because he felt uncomfortable doing all of the jobs his publisher had been doing in the past. He would now be responsible for getting his work edited. He would be responsible for the book cover. He would be responsible for seeing that the interior of the book, the copyright registration, the ISBN, the Library of Congress information, and even the blurbs for the book were taken care of. Just the idea of it all was overwhelming. He almost gave up before he started, but then he got inspired by Yasmin.

Her gig at Louie's Jazz Lounge had been going well, and several members of the house band formed another group to perform more contemporary music in some of the open mic spaces. As a result, this new band, Invisible People, a nod to Ralph Ellison's literary masterpiece, had picked up somewhat of a cult following. That was enough to propel them to release an EP on iTunes and make their music available through a variety of streaming services. Even more, they began to release remixes on SoundCloud for free. Kamal had even seen several people on the streets wearing Invisible People t-shirts. He could hardly conceal a smile when he thought about this. His girlfriend was achieving her dream and developing a bit of fame in a place she had not even lived in for a year.

Kamal figured if the indie approach to art had served Yasmin well, then it might do the same for him. He just needed to finish the novella and begin the tedious process of editing it and getting another set of eyes on it.

He would deal with the cover and all the other things later. At the moment he was just happy to be doing something with his writing that was primarily under his own control. There was no one to stop him, but at the same time, he had no one he could blame if he was unsuccessful.

---

KAMAL HAD BEEN SITTING IN THE DEN WATCHING TV for an hour before he even realized James was in the apartment. It was only when James spoke to him that he jumped, scared out of his wits.

"You need to wear a bell like that one the mice tried to put on the cat. You've got to stop sneaking up on me like that. You're going to give me a heart attack, man!"

James laughed and shrugged his shoulders. "I can't help it. I just don't make a lot of noise when I walk."

"You don't make *any* noise at all when you walk— or even move for that matter."

"Well, I guess so," James said, before sitting down on the love seat perpendicular to the couch Kamal was sitting on.

"What's up?"

"Twan and I are taking a break."

"Whoa," Kamal said, grabbing the remote control and turning off the television. "Are you okay? What happened?"

"This fucking Supreme Court, man."

"I thought legalizing gay marriage was a good thing."

"Yeah," James said. "In general, yes. But now that's all Twan hints at these days."

Kamal chuckled before apologizing. "I know this is not supposed to be funny, but this seems exactly like that Key & Peele sketch where one of the guys in the relationship is reluctant about actually getting married and the other one is gung-ho."

"Yeah, I saw that one. I guess you have a point."

"So what's the problem?"

James leaned back and looked up at the ceiling. "I don't know. It's just that I never thought that marriage would even be an option for me. You might not know this, but my father is a preacher, and he hasn't had much to say to me since I moved out of the house and came to live here in The City. My mother took my coming out a lot better. I mean, she's always sending me care packages, you know.

"I guess part of me thinks that if I got married, then my father and I would never be able to talk again. It feels very permanent."

Kamal nodded. "I see what you mean. But you do love Twan, right?"

"More than anything."

"And he makes you happy?"

"Yes."

"Then why does it matter what your father thinks?" Kamal asked.

James shook his head slowly. "It just does. It's not as black and white as you're painting it. My father is always preaching that marriage is an institution for a man and a woman. He virtually pushes Leviticus down my throat every single time I see him, and when I tell him that there are a lot of so-called sins listed in the same book and that he's cherry-picking verses that fit his own prejudices, he talks about Sodom and Gomorrah and hell fire and how it's supposed to be Adam and Eve, not Adam and Steve. Did you know that Leviticus talks about cutting your hair and having tattoos as sins? Meat with blood in it is a sin, too. My father is such a fucking hypocrite. He shaves religiously, has a tattoo of his fraternity on his arm, and eats every piece of steak he can find medium rare."

Kamal did not know what to say, so he sat silently and gave James space to vent. By the time James finally began to slow down, Kamal calmly pointed out that everything James had talked about had to do with James's father and not Twan.

"I'm not saying that you need to go and get married just because you can, but you can't take out your anger at your father on the one person who truly loves you."

James nodded his head slowly and wiped his eyes. "I don't think you understand, Kamal. There are a million things I can't stand about my dad, but he's still my dad and I love him. And if there is any chance that I will ever be able to sit down with him and have a conversation again, then I have to keep that door open." He sighed heavily. "Things were already perfect with Twan, the time together, the time away from each other. Why did he have to go and mess up a good thing?"

"I'm sure it's not as bad as you think," Kamal responded.

"Bad enough. We argued and argued, and when I wouldn't entertain his ultimatum, he told me that he needed time away from me and this relationship."

Kamal tried not to think of taking sides, but he felt himself leaning more towards sympathizing with Twan. Loving someone was something that was real to him in his life, and not having a father probably left him with little sympathy for trying to appease one who clearly had no problem discarding his own son.

They sat in silence for a while. Finally, James rose to his feet, and like a ghost, he quietly returned to his room, leaving Kamal alone, staring at the turned-off TV screen in front of him.

In that moment, Kamal wondered if Twan was

telling his version of the same story to Yasmin. If so, Twan would probably need to have her close by that night. Kamal took out his phone and texted her.

*James told me about what happened with Twan. If you need to stay over there tonight, I will understand.*

A few seconds later, he received a reply.

*Thank you for understanding. Will call u later?*

He punched in his response. *Sure.*

After he put his phone down, he contemplated turning on the TV or some music, anything to fill the vacuum of silence. Instead, he went back into his bedroom and took out his novella to finish working on it.

## 13

One of the perks of being an adjunct professor was that Kamal would get an educational discount from most of the publishers when he went to buy books. He had already worked out a system for taking advantage of that incentive, too. He would go to bookstores during lunch or immediately after he finished his job at the law firm and take his time combing the bookshelves looking at books from every genre that interested him at the moment. Kamal believed to truly be an effective novelist, you could not confine yourself to reading only fiction. As a result, Kamal's personal library consisted of roughly forty percent nonfiction titles, whether they were cultural, historical, craft, or biographical works. Once he spotted the book he wanted at the bookstore, he would take out his phone and make a quick note of the name of the book, the name of the author, the ISBN of the book, and the name of the publisher. He would shop like this for about an hour, and then take the list home, open his laptop, and go to the individual publishers' websites and order directly from them, using the educational discount. Occasionally, he got the books for free, but normally his discount was one-fourth of the retail price in the stores. By doing this method, Kamal had become quite the bibliophile, with a stack of books so ridiculous he would need an additional lifetime to read them all.

Another perk of being an adjunct professor was that he was often sent free teacher edition textbooks from education publishers. Since he had little say about the actual textbooks he used in the two composition courses he taught, these freebie books served no purpose at all for him, unless he wanted to look through them to see what was useful for supplementing the existing textbooks. What worked much better for him, regarding these free textbooks, was that people would come around periodically throughout the semester to purchase them from him for various textbook companies looking to sell the books directly to students. As a result, Kamal took to collecting these free textbooks and then turning around and selling them for extra cash. It was not the most lucrative of businesses, but a couple hundred here and there gave him a little breathing room on his budget during the month.

When he had first started teaching, the department chair told him they might one day convert his contract to full-time. Although he didn't have a masters degree, he had taken classes for a year, giving him eighteen graduate credits in the field, thereby making him eligible to teach adjunct. He was then led to believe he could be hired full-time based off of his having had two novels published by a major publisher. None of it worked out, though. When a full-time opening did come up, they went with a PhD fresh out of graduate school, a person who had never published anything beyond a modified conference paper in a journal that most people didn't even know existed. When he went back to the department chair to find out what he had to do to make the leap, they told him he needed a terminal degree. Kamal then brought up the question, "What if I went and earned an MFA in Creative Writing? Would that help?" The response was anything but comforting.

"It's better than what you currently have, but if you want to make yourself bullet proof, you'll need to get your PhD. Every single time our committee was given a choice of picking a person with an MFA and a person with a PhD, barring the person with the MFA having won some major award or being a bestseller, we usually went with the PhD. Accreditation-wise, we can get a little more mileage out of the situation. There are a ton of PhD's who are applying for adjunct positions because jobs out there are so scarce. So if you're thinking of going back to school, you might want to look into going for the doctorate," Dr. Patricia Engles, the English department chair, told him.

Kamal took their short talk to mean that he should be thankful that he even had a job, no matter how little it paid, because there were people clearly more qualified than he who did not even have that. That was when he realized that he did not want to commit himself to a life in academia. He was a writer, he knew, and it made no sense for him to bust his ass getting a degree in an area of marginal interest to him.

So Northgovernor College continued to milk him, the published author, for small change, and the published author continued to manipulate the system of bonuses and freebies extended to college professors. Kamal knew one day they would probably not renew his contract, so he trained himself so that he was good at his job, but was never attached to it in any emotional way.

Having that level of detachment gave Kamal more room to focus on building his career as a writer, and one way of doing that was for him to keep writing and to keep reading, thus his regular visits to various bookstores throughout The City, places that rarely, if ever, carried his titles, in spite of Stallings Press being headquartered in The City.

As Kamal moved about the store, he came upon a table of books featuring bestselling authors like Hillary Mantel, Philip Roth, Michael Chabon, Jonathan Franzen, Donna Tart, and Ann Patchett. Every single one of those authors had made a good living and bore critically favorable reputations. They were, of course, also white writers. Even if *The Princess of Fall* was acquired by one of the independent presses he had submitted it to, the book would still never make it to a table like this, one where the publishers clearly had the financial interest and retail display allowance to park his book prominently out there like this.

In that moment, as he stood there both jealous and fascinated, he thought back to the abandoned manuscript tucked away in his desk drawer. The curiosity returned with a vengeance, and Kamal suddenly became intrigued with his idea again. He did not even give himself time to think himself out of it. He knew when he got home that he would start looking for a new literary agent, definitely a white one, and start shopping his book under a pseudonym. It would not hurt anything to at least experiment with it and see if the prospect even had wings. If it didn't work, no harm, no foul. If, however, it did work, maybe, just maybe, he could actually achieve his writing goals at the highest level.

Yes, he would do this. But he would not tell anyone what he was doing, especially not Yasmin.

---

ON THE SUBWAY RIDE BACK TO HIS APARTMENT, Kamal began to revisit possible names to write under. Some names, he was aware, already had cachet built into them, names like Faulkner, Raymond (as a first name), and Flynn. He needed his name to sound like it belonged in that group, without being those exact names. He also did not want an ironic name or any type of moniker that caused the reader to stop for a second and consider the possibility that he or she was looking at something made up.

The name should be able to speak volumes about the writer in a 180 degree difference than his own name could, he reasoned. Then the name hit him like an ice bucket of cold water crashing down over his head.

Kilgore Pickens.

The name was pretty white, Kamal had to admit. It also sounded like the name of a professor of English literature at a university somewhere in New England. It also smacked of Southern aristocracy, which suited Kamal just fine since he was from Mississippi anyway and more aware of the literary legacy of that state than many of his peers at Northgovernor.

He would need a bio for this character, he figured, and by the time he reached his bedroom, he had concocted a background for Kilgore Pickens that smacked of all the things readers of white popular literary fiction would readily embrace. The bio just needed to be short, vague, and mysterious. Having Kilgore be from

Mississippi was a given, so was having him be in his fifties. It would also be more fascinating if he were an autodidact when it came to writing. He could not be an MFA graduate; he had to be a person who worked a career to the point of retirement before discovering that the novel he had been harboring inside of his soul for all those years deserved to see the light of day. He had to be a person who had no family, except for a dog named Rusty. And the two of them lived in an old remodeled antebellum house he inherited, a house that had been in the family for generations. He would embody those mythical traits of Hemingway and Faulkner, while at the same time being a hermit like J.D. Salinger and Thomas Pynchon. In other words, the less you knew about the man, the better. He would communicate with the world through his books, not through social media, interviews, bookstore readings, writing workshops, or even award receptions. He would be an enigma, and Kamal would never have to think about doing anything to market and promote the books, a skill set that he had finally admitted to himself he did not possess anyway.

Kilgore Pickens.

That would work. Now, he just had to change a few more things in the book, including, of course, the title. There was no point in someone who had rejected the title under the name Kamal Jackson to make the connection between him and Kilgore Pickens. There had to be enough of a distance there for people to never really catch on. Plus, Kamal was banking on the fact that those people who had rejected him so quickly had not read beyond the first thirty pages anyway. He would be safe and change the first 100 pages and institute all of the edits that he never sent out to any of the publishers and see if he could get a literary agent to champ at the bit.

He smiled as he opened the drawer to his desk and placed the manuscript in front of himself.

"Good to see you again, old friend," he whispered, turning to the first page of the manuscript.

14

"So how is Twan holding up?" Kamal asked, as he and Yasmin walked through City Park, hand in hand.

"Not so well. Sometimes he seems all right, but other times he gets really depressed."

Kamal gazed out at the skyline framing the outer edges of the park. "I wish James would just go over there already. They clearly love each other. I can't believe they've allowed a week to pass where they haven't even spoken to each other."

"I'm just doing my best to be supportive. Other than that, I'm staying out of his business. He didn't ask me for my input, and I don't have a reason to volunteer it at this point."

"I feel you." It was a bland response, Kamal knew, but he didn't care to talk any more about the subject, if Yasmin had already indicated her desire to not even entertain it. "So, how is everything going with your music?"

"It's cool. When you're indie, you have to work ten times as hard. There's no offline radio station playing us. There are no videos in rotation. In fact, we haven't really made enough money to put a dent in anything.

We're like 'hood famous,'" she said, laughing. "You know that game you played when you were little? Do you want to be rich *or* famous? Sometimes I said one; other times I said the other. I guess I kind of thought they were connected, like beans and rice or peanut butter and jelly, but I was wrong. You can be famous and broke, just like you can be rich and anonymous. I guess you just have to play the hand you're dealt."

"Well, who knows? Maybe your following will bring the big time labels knocking on your door," Kamal said.

Yasmin shrugged her shoulders. "I guess I'm really just happy to have a job—or two. I can figure out the other stuff later. Anything else is just a first world problem."

"What does that mean? First world problem?"

"Those are problems reserved for those who are privileged enough to have them."

Kamal chuckled. "I see. Well, you are fitting in just fine in The City. You're black and you have two jobs. I guess that makes you official then."

Patting her chest with her fist in a mock gesture of pride, she responded, "Gotta represent to the fullest."

"Well, do you think you could represent to the fullest in my bedroom tonight then?" Kamal lifted her hand to his and placed a kiss there.

"You ain't said nothing but a thang. I got you, boo!" Yasmin laughed, snuggling her head against his shoulder. "You don't think we'll make James feel uncomfortable, do you?"

"I doubt it. He pretty much goes in his room when he gets home."

"I'm serious, Kamal. I don't want to put him in a weird space. You know sometimes I can get a little loud."

"James is a big boy. He'll be just fine. I doubt if we would disturb him."

Yasmin stopped walking and stood still. "You should care more about his feelings, you know."

"I do, but right now, I kind of care about the feeling of us getting together. It's been a few days. I don't want what's going on with James and Twan to stop what's going on with us."

Yasmin pondered this for a moment, much to Kamal's surprised. He had assumed that she would see the logic in his suggestion and instantly co-sign on it. Instead, she responded, "Let me think about it, and I'll let you know later. I want to see how Twan is holding up."

"Fair enough," Kamal said, barely able to conceal his disappointment.

They walked over to a bench, just off the walking path, and sat down.

"So how is your novella coming?" Yasmin asked.

"I finished it. Now I'm just letting it breathe before I do an initial edit. I'm also starting to do some research on fonts and formatting. And then there's the cover. I have no idea what I am going to do about that?"

She laid her head on his shoulder and snuggled closer. "What did you have in mind?"

Kamal shifted his weight and allowed her to fall into his embrace. Holding her in his arms, he closed his eyes, trying to imagine what the book should look like. His first novel had a photograph of a pair of shoes on the cover. The second novel had the silhouette of a woman against a rather large, yet colorful font. There was no pattern between the two books, so he had no style to really go after. He had never assumed he would have control over the covers of any of his books, so he had no idea of how he should even go about it. The only thing he knew was that he liked the idea of having a painting or collage on the cover. He had always appreciated art, even more so because he was not artistically-inclined. He could hardly draw a stickman before grabbing an eraser to start over.

"I don't really know. A piece of artwork, like an Ernie Barnes piece—maybe like *The Sugar Shack*—or a Frida Khalo-styled piece."

Yasmin's eyes lit up. "Hey, let me read the novella, and I will come up with something for you."

"You can draw?" Kamal asked.

"I can do a lot of things, Kam."

"Well, see if you can get yourself free this evening."

"I told you that I'll see what I can do. Unless Twan is totally in the basement, I'll be over. How about that?" Yasmin said.

Kamal smiled and nodded his head. "I can get with that."

They rested quietly, taking in the random people around them: joggers, kids chasing balloons, and nannies pushing strollers. In the whirlwind of his own thoughts, Kamal reminded himself that he needed to remember to put *The Princess of Fall* away this time. He didn't want it to inadvertently kill Yasmin's mood.

"A penny for your thoughts," she asked, bringing him back into the moment.

"I'm just happy to be here with you."

"Same here," she responded, interlocking her fingers with his. "You're good people."

"Why do you say that?"

"Because I know you would never do anything to hurt me."

It seemed like such a strange thing to randomly blurt out, Kamal thought, but he only nodded his agreement, momentarily pushing his Kilgore Pickens novel from his mind. "I could never hurt you."

---

By eleven o'clock that evening Kamal had not heard from Yasmin. He assumed things with Twan might have been too extreme for her to leave. He had texted her several times and gotten no response. She probably wouldn't be coming through, he figured.

To take his mind off of her, he logged onto the *Poets & Writers* website and started combing through a list of literary agents. He scanned through numerous profiles, and the ones that stood out to him, he cross-referenced with Google to see if he could get a list of the authors they represented. He had already copied and pasted information for ten agents who represented authors who had won Pulitzers, Man Booker Prizes, and even two MacArthur Genius fellowship recipients. The clients for these agents also had the elite teaching positions throughout the country, spending their summers running workshops for Breadloaf or some top-notch writing foundation.

Kamal's phone buzzed violently against the mahogany of his desk, and he quickly glanced down at it. It was Yasmin.

"Hello?"

"You're still up?" she asked.

"Yeah. Is everything okay?"

"I'm good. I fell asleep after getting an early dinner with Twan. He's still in his funk, but he's doing better. If you want me to, I can still come over."

Kamal glanced at the clock on his computer. It was a few minutes to midnight. He had already gotten into a groove with his research and had reconciled himself to the fact that he would not be seeing Yasmin that night. He considered telling her that they could just get together tomorrow, but he knew his mindset would easily shift once she walked through the door. There was a part of him that worried for her safety with her traveling that late at night, though.

"Would it be better if I came over there? I don't feel comfortable getting you into a cab this late at night by yourself."

"A gentleman. And in The City? I need to write a song about that," she responded, laughing. "Seriously, I can come to you."

"Yaz, I'm not taking 'no' for an answer. If you want to see me, and you don't think it'll be a problem with Twan, let me come over there tonight. I can be quiet. If you don't scream, I shole won't holler," he said, referring to that Bill Nunn line from the *School Daze* post-swimsuit party scene.

"What would you do to me tonight?" she asked, her voice softening, the coyness dripping from her lips with each syllable.

"I have been fantasizing about the taste of you all day."

"So you want to taste me?"

"Uh-huh. You like that?"

"Yes."

"Hey, we can do this all night, but wouldn't you rather me use my mouth on you directly. I'm just saying. You're only fifteen minutes away. There's no need to fantasize when you can have me over there showing and proving."

Yasmin took a deep breath. "Okay. Hurry up and come."

"I'll do that, but just don't say that phrase to me

after I get there. I really want to take my time with you tonight."

Yasmin chuckled softly. "I'll be listening for you, so knock softly. I don't want to wake up Twan."

"No problem. I'll see you in a few minutes."

When Kamal hung up the phone, he looked at his laptop and saved the names of the literary agents he had highlighted. He would query each of them tomorrow. But that was tomorrow.

It was all about Yasmin tonight, he thought, his body already buzzing with anticipation.

STRAINING TO BE QUIET, KAMAL'S AND YASMIN'S bodies, soaked in sweat, pushed and pulled against each other, seeking friction amidst the wetness that threatened to engulf them both. When Yasmin came, her mouth pressed hard into the pillow next to her face, she screamed in pure ecstasy. With her body still contracting in the throws of orgasm, she demanded that Kamal climax. "Now!" she whispered with such ferocity that Kamal felt his body swell with the glow of the most extreme pleasure he had ever experienced. He reached beneath her bottom and lifted her hips into him, as he extended his thrusts deep into her, his abdominal muscles on the verge of cramping, just as her fingernails raked softly across his stomach. He looked down into her face, the perspiration on her face causing the hair strands across her forehead to lie there, plastered as if she had lifted her face to a rainstorm. She was not just beautiful; she was intensely sexy. "Now," she commanded again.

This time he surrendered.

THE WETNESS FORCED THEM TO CHANGE THE sheets before they went to sleep. They took turns drying each other off with one of the towels Yasmin had brought into her room before he arrived. When they were as dry as they could be, given the circumstances, they lay down and turned out the lamps. Alone in the dark, they cuddled beneath the fresh, cool sheets.

His eyes closed, Kamal could feel his body buzzing, as if it wanted to float up and touch the ceiling. *I could lie here forever*, he thought, rubbing his palm over Yasmin's hip. She moaned softly and backed herself against him so that their bodies were pressed firmly against each other.

"I love you," he whispered, before he could catch himself. He had been thinking it for a few months now, but he did not know how and when the words would escape his lips. He had assumed it would be at a time other than one of post-coital bliss.

"What did you say?" Yasmin said, turning to face him.

Kamal could scarcely make out her face in the dark and wondered if she could really see him or if she just wanted to be facing him to better understand him.

"I said that I love you."

"Wow."

"That's all you have to say? Did I say the wrong thing?"

"No, not at all. I'm just a bit surprised. That's all."

Kamal chuckled, trying to mask his incredulity. "We have been together for over six months. I figured that it was obvious—with you being my girl and all."

"Your girl?"

Kamal sat up in his bed, confused. "You're joking, right? Don't play with me right now."

Yasmin reached over and turned on the lamp next to her bed. "I'm not playing with you, Kam. We never talked about being in a relationship, so I'm just trying to process what you're saying. That's all."

"You've got to be shitting me!" he responded, trying to keep his voice low, but unable to conceal the thumping emotion beneath his words. "We've been together the entire time you have been in The City. Why are you acting all brand new? Are you dating someone else besides me? Is that it?"

Yasmin shook her head. "You're the only person I'm going out with, but I'm not really the relationship type. I thought we were just kicking it. Buddies, you know?"

Kamal stood up from the bed and stared at her. "I don't even know who you are right now. How could you not know that we're together?"

"Well, we've never had a conversation about it. I never agreed to be in a committed relationship with you."

"But you're fucking me exclusively, I'm assuming."

"Yeah. I'm not a ho."

"So you don't love me then."

Yasmin shrugged her shoulders. "I guess I never really thought about it."

Kamal stared at Yasmin for a long moment before he realized that he was standing there nude in front of her, looking silly. "Maybe I should leave," he finally said.

"That's up to you. I'd like you to stay, though."

"I swear I don't know who you are anymore," he repeated.

Yasmin sat on the edge of the bed, facing him. "Don't be like that. We have a good thing going."

Kamal stood up, his eyebrow arching involuntarily. Where had he heard that before? Dammit, James had said the same thing about Twan. The fucking irony of all ironies. Or was it a coincidence? Who fucking cared?

"I'm leaving."

"If you have to go, you have to do what you have to do."

Putting on his clothes, he glanced back at Yasmin and repeated for the third time that he didn't know who she was anymore.

"Kam," she finally responded, "I'm not trying to make this any more difficult than it already is, but I have to wonder if you *ever* really knew who I was in the first place by everything you're saying."

"Maybe you're right," he said, walking out of her room.

## 15

The following day Kamal called in sick, taking a sick day he did not really have available to take in the first place. He just couldn't managed the energy to rise from his bed. He replayed the entire six months of his relationship with Yasmin, searching for clues that she had been feeling differently about things than he had. Every single scene he could bring to mind revealed two people romantically connected and intimately involved. There were the public displays of affection, the intense lovemaking sessions, the deep and meaningful conversations that they had at night, the genuine concern they showed for each other, and the friendship they had that seemed to be the type of friendship many couples would have killed for. They were perfect in his mind. How could she have been thinking anything different than he had? She had experienced everything that he had and somehow come out on an entirely different wavelength. If she was dating someone else, it would have made more sense to him, but being that she was exclusive without being committed, he was completely unable to wrap his mind around what was happening.

Whether or not he could comprehend what had

happened, he knew that he was now alone. How do you come back from something like this? He desperately tried to make sense of it all. And it was not just the sex or the time together. He had just lost his closest friend. He couldn't help but dwell on what he couldn't understand or change.

His phone continued to vibrate throughout the morning with phone calls and text messages. He assumed them all to be from Yasmin and never looked at the phone screen. He needed a moment to process what was happening, and he was in no mental state to talk to her about anything, let alone what it was that they could mutually agree that the two of them shared.

When he finally rolled out of bed, he walked into the kitchen and made a huge bowl of cereal. James's door was closed, so he returned to his room and sat down at his writing desk. He opened his laptop and pulled up the list of literary agents he had compiled the night before.

The first on the list was a guy named Carson Matthews. Carson currently represented several authors who were on Kamal's shelf. Interestingly, none of those authors were writers of color, although one had won a Pulitzer and another had been a finalist twice for a National Book Critics Circle Award. One thing Kamal noticed about the writers Carson Matthews signed, however, was that they were primarily rugged men who wrote with stark imagery and forceful, short sentences. Carson clearly had a hard-on for Ernest Hemingway and sought male writers who wrote in that same vein. He wondered briefly if Carson could even punctuate a complex sentence containing an appositive. It was clear that he didn't have many writers who used them, so who knew? Still, he decided to send his manuscript to Carson, figuring that the agent was long overdue for representing a writer with style that had little resemblance to Hemingway's.

The next name on the list was Mary Beth Huntington. Mary Beth had an extensive client list that included two Orange Prize winners and a Man Booker finalist. Many of her clients were women, but there were a few men in the mix, most of whom Kamal had never heard of. The thing he liked most about Mary Beth was that she represented writers who were excellent storytellers, writers who didn't get lost in trying to prove their technical prowess. Clearly, she had an excellent eye for stories that embodied a universal appeal, as even her English authors were American bestsellers, too. He would submit his manuscript to her, as well.

Nisha Patel was next on the list. While her agency page included some really impressive clients, most of whom were white, as opposed to South Asian or any other ethnic group in the diaspora, Kamal found it difficult to really find a great deal of information about her on the Internet. Her name was so popular that he had to scroll through pages and pages of doctors, models, executives, restauranteurs, and hospitality specialists, all accomplished women in their own right, all with the same name. For Nisha to be Indian, she seemed to be plugged into a white dominated publishing industry very well. He respected her for this and wondered if she would be a good ally in the cause. He sent her his novel.

Kamal continued down the list, making notes about each of the literary agents. In the end, he decided to create a new email account for Kilgore Pickens and send out queries to all of them. He was starting over from scratch, and he knew any one of these agents could do wonders for his (or Kilgore's) career.

He glanced at the clock on his computer. It was a

little after 10:00 a.m., so he walked back out into the den area to see if James had awakened. James's door was open and he was gone. Like a ghost, he had once again gone *poof!* Then Kamal remembered that James's play had a special show time that day at two o'clock in the afternoon. They did this every Wednesday, but Kamal had never been to a show during that time, mainly because he had to work during those hours.

Kamal headed back to his room and picked up his phone. There were eight text messages from Yasmin, four missed calls, and two voicemails. A person would have thought she was a jilted fiancee by the unembarrassed persistence she employed in trying to contact him. Without reading her messages, he sent a text to James to see if he could leave a ticket for him at the Will Call window for the two o'clock show. He then put his phone down and went into the bathroom to get ready for the day.

---

THE SUBWAY RIDE DOWNTOWN WAS UNEVENTFUL, so Kamal took out his phone and started reading the text messages from Yasmin.

He looked at the first one.

*Wow. What just happened?*

Then the next.

*I had no idea you felt that way. It just kind of caught me off guard.*

The next.

*I do care about you. Just wanted you to know that, in case you were wondering.*

The next.

*Are you ignoring my texts? I just left a voicemail. Please tell me what's going on.*

The next.

*You're gonna to throw away our friendship over a misunderstanding? I didn't think you were that type of person.*

The next.

*Sorry about the last text. I'm trippin'.*

The next.

*Okay. I get it. I'll leave you alone.*

And finally the last text.

*I don't use the word love lightly. I want it to be special when I use it. Hope you are well. Peace.*

By the time Kamal arrived at the Franklin Theater, he had read all of the text messages several times each. The last one resonated with him the most, though. There seemed to be some kind of awareness that their relationship was actually special. Maybe he'd been premature in walking out on her. Whatever the two of them needed to say to each other, he figured, should be said face-to-face, not via text messages or telephone calls or voicemails. He needed to be able to look into her eyes and feel where she was coming from. He had to be able to sense the meanings in between the words. It was pointless going back and forth with text messages when their meanings were often misinterpreted at worst or muted at best.

James had left a ticket at the Will Call window, and Kamal walked in and took a seat in the third row from the stage. Even at two o'clock in the afternoon, the theater was a little over three quarters full. Kamal looked around at all of the people of various ages and ethnicities sitting in the audience and wondered why any of them were able to see a play at this time of day. He, himself, was only there because he had called in sick, but he wondered if these people even had jobs. Maybe there were a few millionaires in the room, a few people who worked evening shifts, a few people on vacation, a few professors who taught on alternating days, and maybe the rest were tourists. He didn't know, but he felt his guesses were solid, nonetheless.

One of the theater workers made a statement about no photography in the theater, and then the lights dimmed three times before going completely dark. The stage curtains opened, revealing the realistic cut-out of a large brick building. A table and three chairs sat out in front of the building, and a man and woman sat facing each other. The woman was Latina, and the guy was white. They were having breakfast on what appeared to be one of the closed off streets in The City that tourists used to sit and drink coffee and eat bagels. Several other people stood around in the background, some taking pictures and staring at things, tourist-style. There was a hot dog vendor off to the side, and beneath the vendor's hat was James.

Throughout much of the first half of the play, Kamal could not really follow what was going on. It all seemed too abstract—not to mention boring. By the time the lights came up for intermission, Kamal was deep in his own thoughts. They oscillated back and forth between his Kilgore Pickens strategy and his questionable status with Yasmin. He looked at his phone and considered texting her to let her know that he had received all of her messages and that they should meet up, but then the lights dimmed three times, and he found his way back to the seat. The theater went dark again, and the curtains opened to the same set.

Not wanting to be disrespectful to the actors, he struggled to keep his eyes open. And he was glad that he had, because five minutes after the play continued, James walked to the center of the stage and gave a monologue. It was odd, disjointed, full of exposition, and confusing, but James delivered it with such passion that Kamal could not look away. Once the monologue was completed, James returned to his hot dog cart and did not say anything else for the rest of the play.

When the play was finally over, two hours and forty minutes after it had begun, Kamal waited outside the theater for his roommate.

Roughly half an hour later, James emerged in street clothes, floating in his usual stroll.

"So what did you think?" James asked, his lips twisted into a funky smile.

"You were good!"

"I know this," he responded, laughing. "Thank you. But what I wanted to know is if the *play* was any good."

"Well, to be honest," Kamal said, "I didn't really understand it."

"Roomie, let me be honest with you. I don't understand a lick of that shit myself. I just do my part to make it as interesting as I can."

Kamal laughed.

As they walked down the street, James continued. "It's a gig. And it pays. Plus, I get Equity benefits, so I will stand behind that damn hot dog cart as long as they want me to."

Kamal nodded. "What exactly was the play *supposed* to be about?"

"I have no goddamn clue. I think it's about existential crises in The City. Hell, I don't know. I just think about what Russell Crowe said when he was doing *The Gladiator*. He said the script was shit, but he was great actor and could make shit look good."

"Hah! He actually said that? I like that movie!" Kamal responded.

They walked to a coffee shop four blocks down

from the theater and grabbed the only free table in the back of the place.

"I heard about you and Yasmin," James said.

Kamal frowned, wondering exactly how that information had gotten out so quickly. Then he realized that Twan must have talked to James and told him everything that he had overheard last night.

"So you and Twan are talking again?" Kamal asked.

"Yeah. He said that you and Yasmin had a disconnect and you stormed out of the apartment last night. You all right? I know that you guys are pretty serious."

"I thought we were. We were having a great evening, cuddling in bed, you know, and I told her that I loved her. Then she started trippin' out. Turns out that she thinks of me more as an exclusive fuck buddy than a boyfriend."

James shook his head. "Damn. I didn't see that one coming. You guys are like frick and frack, thick as thieves. Frankly, I'm surprised you guys didn't profess your love to each other months ago."

"That's what *I'm* saying. I figured six months was more than enough time to come clean about how I was feeling. But, you know, if I had never said anything, I would have been blissfully ignorant, walking around in this bubble of misunderstanding every single time I was with her."

"That's a tough one," James said.

A server came to the table to take their orders. They both ordered coffees.

"I'll survive," Kamal said, "but tell me about you and Twan. Have you guys gotten over your differences?"

"We're working on it. I'm still not a hundred percent on this marriage thing, but I do want us to be together, and so does he. We're going to just take our time with things and stay open to the possibilities."

"So does that mean you'll be spending the night over there on your regular schedule?" Kamal joked.

"We'll see. We're just taking it a day at a time. I haven't ruled out marriage at this point."

Kamal patted James on the shoulder. "Do I hear some evolution in your thinking?"

"I'm still torn, I'm not going to lie, but I am starting to think that my relationship with my father is a two-way street. He should be willing to meet me halfway, but as of today, he hasn't budged an inch. I can't do this all by myself, and I can't live my life with a huge 'what if' hanging over my head like a pendulum."

Kamal nodded. "I feel you."

"So have you decided what you're going to do about Yasmin?"

"Sorta kinda." Kamal paused. "Not really."

James poked out his lips in thought. "I'm not offering any suggestions to what you should do, but I figured it wouldn't hurt to tell you the little bit that I know about Yasmin, since I've known her a tad bit longer than you."

Kamal sat silently, completely attentive.

"She's a genuine person. She's not a bullshitter—at all. That's definitely one of the things that stands out about her the most. She doesn't try to be something that she's not, and because she's always real about who she is and how she moves in the world, you never have to second guess her or think there's some ulterior motive to her words or actions. In a place like The City, that's a rare trait to have. Now whether the two of you work everything out is on you, but I would treat everything she tells you, for better or worse, as the truth, as far as she is concerned."

Kamal considered this, placing what James said about her with the experiences he had had with her over the past six months. James's assessment was spot-on with his own. The only thing about a person being so direct and straight-up is that it sometimes accompanies a truth that you might not want to hear.

"She left me a few messages. I need to call her back and see if we can just sit down and talk it out."

"A few messages? It sounds like she really wants to talk to you."

"Yeah. I want to talk to her, too."

James took another sip of coffee and placed it on the table. He removed his wallet from his pocket and put enough cash on the table to cover both coffees and a tip. "So why are you sitting here? You should be trying to talk to Yasmin."

Kamal nodded his head, thanked James for the coffee and the ticket to the play, and headed out into The City, his cell phone already dialing Yasmin's phone number.

## 16

The idea for *The Princess of Fall* originated with a dream Kamal had while visiting his mother in Mississippi, shortly before she up and decided she'd had enough of the racism in her late husband's home state and moved to a cottage in the countryside of Worcester, England. Kamal rarely saw his mother much these days, but she sent Christmas cards like clockwork, always asking him to keep her in the loop should he ever decide to settle down with a nice young lady and have some children.

The idea had come after he spent the afternoon that August driving around on the back roads throughout the county. He had marveled at how spaced out the houses were once you left the city limits. It wasn't uncommon to see a house situated on nine or ten acres of land by itself, the closest neighbor nearly two hundred yards away. It was nothing like the suburban subdivisions where large McHouses sprang up so close together that next door neighbors nearly shared the same driveway. These country houses gave new meaning to going to ask your neighbor for a cup of sugar, for that walk might be considered by city dwellers to be an actual trek.

Fields punctuated the landscape: a corn field here, a soy bean field there. Greens galore: collards, mustards, turnips. And then there was the cotton—a crop that gave Kamal the willies every time he saw one of the fields, those white fluffy cotton boles bursting from their prickly cells. Every time he saw a field of cotton, he thought about his ancestors toiling away under an unforgiving Mississippi sun, plucking away from *can't see in the morning* to *can't see at night.* It was the corn, however, that arrested his attention on his afternoon drive that day.

The stalks were high enough that they would exceed even his own height of five foot eleven inches, and he immediately imagined an adolescent girl who might have grown up on a farm like that and what she would do to pass the time, since it was very likely that her closest neighbor in age was miles away. Then it hit him: she would dance—and what better place to dance privately than buried in the crops that enveloped your home?

As he considered this image, he imagined the little girl's father, a man of earnest means, a widower, struggling to rear his only child amidst a farm that threatened to choke out his own creativity. What would a man like that really want to do if he had the means to improve his circumstances?

Kamal navigated the two lane highway from memory, although he had not driven on it for more than ten years. The land was flat, with the occasional hill there to break up the monotony, the crests in the road just enough to give the vehicle's engine a slight bit of exercise. It was a place he was used to, but he wondered how a person from another country, like say Germany, in the region of Bavaria, might view such a landscape. By the time Kamal laid his head upon the pillow in his childhood bedroom that night, he knew exactly what the old widower would have wanted to do if he could get out from under his farm: he would build a castle! He would raze his field and build a castle where the corn once stood.

It was a *Field of Dreams* kind of idea, but there were multiple layers of complexity embedded within: parenthood, loneliness, the need to reinvent oneself, Southern culture, the farming culture, and on and on.

And no Southern story could be told without a ghost or some element of the macabre. The story would definitely embody traces of the gothic. It was the story that any Mississippian would recognize, but it was also a story that anyone who lived outside the region would be blown away by. Kamal took copious notes and left the idea alone.

Years later, after he had already published his first novel, *Dope Revolution*, and was in the middle of writing *A Junkyard of Absurdities*, his latest published novel, he had the hankering to return to this new novel set on a farm in Mississippi. It was almost as if the novel was demanding to be written.

A year after the publication of *A Junkyard of Absurdities*, Kamal had completed the first draft of *The Princess of Fall*. It was, in his humble opinion, his best work to date, the one that would define him as a Southern novelist to reckon with, the one that would secure his place in the canon of Southern literature, the one that would show the world what he was capable of doing upon the page.

Even in the narrow and elite space of literary novels, Kamal felt, perhaps with a bit too much hubris at times, that his novel deserved a seat at that table. But the novel did not fit with what publishers (and maybe even readers) wanted from an African-American author. The acceptable subject matter for African-American authors, while making room for urban adventures; erotic dick-slinging, melodramatic love stories; slavery; and civil rights, did not seem to have a designation for stories that were set in Southern life in a way that did not revolve around race. The only African American he knew who could write those types of works and still get published was Percival Everett, and Kamal, according to Vanessa Travont, was likely no Percival Everett either.

Kilgore Pickens did not have to entertain such headaches. He was an older white man from Mississippi and could write anything he wanted, however he chose to do so. His offbeat characters and simplistic writing style would be viewed as evidence of his recently excavated genius. Even more, his unwillingness to embrace the spotlight afforded by independent and chain bookstores, as well as literary magazines and the larger writing community, would quietly allow him to absorb an air of the mysterious, antisocial, yet wise, white male writer.

Kilgore's white maleness was important because few readers gave a damn about hermits who were anything other than white males (Harper Lee having once been the most notable exception). There was no writer of color equivalent in the United States, nor was there a woman writer, white or otherwise, who stoked that degree of interest from the larger literary reading public, except for maybe Agatha Christie, who had to disappear for that to even happen.

Kamal considered these things when he fired off his queries, and as a result, he crafted the letter in such a way that any industrious literary agent might feel that he or she was on the verge of discovering the "next big thing," something each of them privately (and not so privately) wanted, but was difficult to achieve in a publishing climate that demanded bestsellers to placate the shareholders of the publicly traded companies that owned the publishing houses.

If no one responded, his experiment would be over, and he would consider self-publishing the novel, assuming the novella he was on the verge of putting out did anything remotely interesting in that space.

The fate of the book rested in the hands of one of the ten literary agents on the receiving end of the query. While the number was small, Kamal felt he would do better by focusing on ten individuals effectively, rather than focus on a boat load of them without regard to personal preferences and interests. These literary agents had been handpicked. Surely one of them had to take the bait.

## 17

After texting Yasmin and even calling and leaving a voicemail for her, Kamal still had been unable to catch up with her. These days, with her two jobs, he knew his best bet was to keep patient and wait for her to return his phone call once she had a free minute. After all, it seemed like she was always gigging, either for Louie's or for The Invisible People. She was committed to her grind. Could that have been one of the reasons she hadn't considered that he might grow emotionally attached to her? Kamal didn't know what to think anymore. His feelings had not diminished any since the last time they spoke; still, he remained stubbornly optimistic that Yasmin would come over to his way of thinking. For him to move to her side would require him to abandoned everything his heart told him about her. Still, he momentarily entertained the idea of just being involved with her without all of his feelings rolling off his body in waves. Could he just be her fuck buddy?

The day seemed to stretched out infinitely slow, his phone almost as useless as if it had been dropped in a public toilet. Lying in bed, near midnight, he picked up his phone again and tried calling Yasmin. When he didn't get her, he left an awkward voicemail, telling her that he missed talking to her and hoped she would give him a call so they could talk all of this "stuff" out. An hour later, still not having heard from her, he texted her with one of the "goodnight kiss" text messages he had been sending her for months. Normally when he did this, she would respond within a few minutes with a brief note of her own. Tonight, however, his phone continued to lie dormant, as if it were the only phone not connected to a cellular network, this idle piece of metal and plastic, nothing more than a toy, where for its owner to have a conversation, he would have to engage with his own imagination to his heart's content.

KAMAL AWOKE THE NEXT MORNING TO A PHONE that had not rung all night. There was no text message awaiting him, but as he scanned through his Kilgore Pickens emails, three of the ten literary agents he had queried requested copies of the full manuscript. He hadn't anticipated a thirty percent response rate. Honestly, a ten percent (or one single response from a literary agent) would have been an amazing accomplishment. After all, he had only submitted his query to a handful for literary agents, an uncommon practice, as far as he had researched, not that different from a person applying to only three colleges, all of which were in the applicant's top tier choices.

The three agents to respond were Carson Matthews, Blair Atkins, and Jeffrey McDonald, three white men. Kamal wondered if there was something in particular in his query that caused the women agents to not respond. Still, landing an email from Carson Matthews's agency was a wonderful piece of good fortune, since Carson was perhaps the most accomplished literary agent out of the entire list Kamal sent his queries to.

He quickly responded to the emails, attaching a Word document of his fully edited manuscript to each of them, and crossed his fingers, hoping that the manuscript could live up to the hype of the query.

In the meantime, Kamal readied himself for work and hopped on the subway headed downtown. Because he lived so far away from his job, nearly the entire morning commute took place underground in a packed tube of other people who were not totally unlike himself: people dressed in inexpensive business attire, headed to office jobs where seniority was judged by how close your cubicle was to the window.

When he emerged from underground, he found himself floored by the beauty of the winter morning, the crisp air with a blue sky holding isolated clouds tenderly and serenely. It was the kind of day that tempted him to play hooky, but he had already done that recently and needed to keep his job, so playing by the rules going forward was a must.

He entered the lobby of his office building and took the elevator to the fifteenth floor, where he proceeded to swipe his card on the wall outside the glass doors of the reception area. The signal on the wall swiper flashed red, as opposed to its normal green light. He looked down at his card and rotated it in his hand, before wiping it back and forth on the thigh of his khakis. Again, he tried and the light flashed red. He looked at the door to make sure he had gotten off the elevator on the correct floor and was standing in front of the correct law firm (lord knows there were plenty of them in the building). He swiped his card again and again and again, a red light flashing each time, the door remaining locked. Finally, he pushed the buzzer beside the card swiper and waited for Angie Duval, the receptionist, to answer and buzz him in. Maybe they changed the cards while he was away.

"Yes," she responded calmly.

Kamal didn't need to tell her who he was because he knew she could see him on the video monitor at her desk, but he did so anyway. "Angie, it's me, Kamal. Can you buzz me in? My ID card isn't working."

"Hold on for a moment," Angie responded.

Kamal waited for the door to buzz open, but it didn't. Two minutes later, his office manager, Calvin Bricks, appeared at the door with one of the guys who worked security. He was holding a single box.

The security guy opened the door and Calvin stepped through with the box, handing it directly to Kamal.

"Your services here are no longer required. We have already contacted your temp agency and you can follow up with their human resources department to determine what happens from here?"

"What's going on?" Kamal asked, unable to conceal his confusion.

"Just as I said. This gentleman here," Calvin said, pointing to the security guy, "will escort you down to the lobby. Sorry it didn't work out."

"Hey, wait, Calvin. Can you at least tell me what I did wrong?"

Clearly wanting to be done with the matter, Calvin sighed and turned to face Kamal. "You can't just call in sick on the most important day of the quarter, especially when you're only a temp." With that, he turned around and went back into the office, the glass doors locking closed behind him.

The security guy followed Kamal downstairs into

the lobby, an embarrassingly unnecessary gesture, as far as Kamal was concerned, but he complied, not wanting to make a scene. That was not who he was. He wanted to maintain some semblance of dignity in spite of his being fired. After all, he was a writer, not a jack of all trades for a law firm. He vowed that his former bosses would one day read his words (after having paid for them, of course) and that he would get the last laugh.

He stepped back at into the morning, the sky suddenly not looking as amazing as it had only minutes earlier. He was now left with one job that did not pay him enough to keep up with his rent. Although he hated to, he knew he would likely have to borrow from James next month and see if he qualified for unemployment checks. With only six thousand dollars as a payment for the semester for teaching two composition classes, Kamal had officially entered a state of poverty. He needed to find something to do immediately before he could actually feel the fear and destitution that accompanied it, though.

Again, he picked up his phone and tried calling Yasmin. He really needed to talk to her, to hear her voice. He assumed that she would be home since much of her work was done at night and she usually slept through the morning. When she did not answer, he decided to take the subway up to Twan's apartment. Remembering how she had waited outside for him on his brownstone when she first arrived in The City, he figured it might be okay for him to do the same, if it just so happened that she was not there.

Twan lived in a ritzy little neighborhood on the upper west side of The City, an area that was known for its art museums and great shopping. It was also a trendy place with a few swanky bars, a high-end grocery store that catered to people who only ate free-range chicken with no growth hormones and drank bottled smoothies with lemongrass in them. It was a place Kamal envied but could not have afforded unless he was already successful. This was not the neighborhood for *aspiring* artists; it was the neighborhood for those who were successfully doing the damn thing.

Kamal walked up the street to Twan's apartment building and pushed the buzzer by the door. It was the second buzzer he had pressed that morning. He only hoped that he would not be shut out of this place, too.

"Hello?" he heard Twan's voice answer.

"Hey, Twan. This is Kamal. I was wondering if you could buzz me in."

Rather than respond, Kamal could hear the buzzer ring out and the door unlock. He walked up to the second set of doors and the buzzer rang again, with that set of doors unlocking, too.

He quickly ascended the stairs and walked down the hall of the second floor to the last apartment on the right. The door was already cracked open.

When he pushed it open, he was greeted by Twan.

"Hey," he whispered. "Yaz is sleeping in her room. She calls herself being mad at you, and I know she would probably kick my ass for letting you in, but I feel like you guys need to fix what's going on between the two of you. If James and I can fix our situation, then you guys have no excuses," he said, a slight smile on his face. "You get a pass this one time. If she tells me that she doesn't want to see you after today, I'm going to have to respect my cousin's wishes. Understood?"

Kamal nodded. "Thanks, man. I owe you one."

"Don't promise me anything too soon. You have some damage to repair before you can say that."

Kamal stood there, nodding, humbled by the morning's events so far.

"Well, don't just stand there. Go and see if you can make my cousin happy."

Kamal smiled and reached out, hugging Twan.

"Go on with all of that," Twan responded, smiling.

Kamal walked over to Yasmin's closed door and knocked lightly. When she didn't answer, he gently cracked open the door, half-expecting to see a guy lying in bed with her. Instead, what he saw was Yasmin sleeping on her side, hugged up with a large pillow in the spot where Kamal normally slept.

He walked around to her side of the bed and stood behind her. He whispered her name, and she did not stir. He then decided to just lie down in the bed beside her. When she did not stir, he whispered in her ear. "I know you are awake, and I know that you probably don't want to see me right now, but I just wanted to let you know that I miss you. I miss you so much that my heart aches. You are my best friend. I'm sorry if I lost it the other night. I just care about you so much, and it stung me that you might not feel the same way. But being without you over these past few days has taught me something. It's taught me that I want you in my life any way that I can possibly get you and that I will love you regardless of if it takes you twenty years to say the same thing to me—if you ever do. If you want me to leave, just tell me. If you want me to stay, just let me know."

For a second, she did nothing, and Kamal began to think she really was asleep. Finally, she backed herself up into his body, moaned softly, and grabbed his hand, placing it across her hip.

Kamal's body filled with a strange and wonderful warmth. He had lost his job, but he had not lost everything. There was still this beautiful woman who was willing to give him a chance to be something special to her, and he found himself unable to speak. He closed his eyes and leaned his face next to hers. Kissing the nape of her neck, he felt his insides glow with that amorous feeling that had come to define his feelings for her.

"Thank you," she whispered, her voice so soft he almost missed it.

He kissed her again and lay back down beside her. Within minutes, he, too, had fallen asleep.

---

By the time Yasmin rose from the bed to get her shower, Twan had already left to meet with a B-list actor about style consultation. Kamal sat up in bed, eagerly watching her undress and grab her robe.

"Want some company?" he asked.

Yasmin did not respond. She only lowered her robe and walked out of the room, leaving the door ajar behind her. Kamal hopped out of bed and followed her around to the bathroom, which was situated nearly identical to the location in his and James's apartment. The door to the bathroom was cracked open, the shower already running. He quickly disrobed and pulled back the shower curtains, entering the warmth of the water and Yasmin's embrace.

They did not talk, at least not with their mouths. She touched him, and he touched her, and it was as if neither had ever experienced the magnificent bliss of the other's body until that moment. Kisses and erotic touches awakened Kamal's urges to be completely enveloped by her, her wetness inviting him to a place that he so sorely missed.

Their sexual enthusiasm almost caused Kamal to come tumbling out of the shower and onto the floor when they moved into an intense position and he almost lost his footing in the tub. Once he regained his composure, Yasmin laughed heartily at his reflex-filled recovery. His heart still beating rapidly from nearly slamming against the floor, coupled with his embarrassment, caused him to move more slowly, more deliberately, and it was those actions that helped to bring Yasmin to climax much faster.

They finished their lovemaking in tact and proceeded to wash each other with the body wash sitting on the edge of the tub. It was almost reverential, their movements, the gentle way their hands moved over the other's body, the thick aromatic lather kissing their skin, fingers delighting and sliding through the suds as water sprinkled down like a spring rain rinsing them clean.

As they stood, drying each other with one large bath towel, Kamal wanted to ask Yasmin what she was thinking, but he decided to let things be as they were. He was happy to be connected to her again, and for that, he did not require an explanation of any kind.

## 19

After getting dressed and walking down to the diner at the end of the block, Kamal and Yasmin began the process of reconciling their situation by sharing what had transpired in the days they were apart from each other. Yasmin's world had continued on as it had before their falling out: she worked and wrote music and practiced and did other promotional activities in relation to both of her bands. It was if she had only become more focused when Kamal was not there. Kamal, on the other hand, had lost his job, which he described in an entertaining, somewhat exaggerated anecdote that fell just shy of him being thrown onto the sidewalk in front of the building. It was the making of what would become a success story in The City, that is if he were ever to become successful, he joked.

Yasmin took his losing his job much harder than he did. Having been fired from her first job at Red Lobster in Memphis, Tennessee, years ago, she still felt a certain empathy for those who were fired without any advanced warning whatsoever. It was only after he reassured her that the law firm had done him a favor by forcing him to get more serious about his writing that she reluctantly co-signed on his comment and began the process of encouraging him to continue focusing on his writing.

Kamal wanted to tell her about the emails he had received from the literary agents he queried, but he didn't want to broach the subject of Kilgore Pickens. He remembered how she had reacted when she saw his edited manuscript. They were just now getting back on good terms, and he didn't want to do anything to derail that. He decided to limit his update to just his being fired.

"Have you published your novella yet?" she asked.

Even though it had only been a few days, hearing her phrase the question like that made the time passage feel much longer.

"Not yet," he replied. "I still need a cover."

Yasmin smiled. "I'll have one for you before the week is out. Then you have to promise me that you will go ahead and make a move with that."

"We'll see."

She placed a hand on his. "I just want to see you do well."

"I know," he responded. "And I appreciate that. I just need to get on my grind. I have all the time in the world right now to focus on my writing without a day job in place."

Yasmin nodded. "Who knows what will happen? I was reading online that there are a number of people who have been able to self-publish so well that they do it full-time. No outside employment at all. It would be cool if you were one of those people who became wildly successful like that."

Kamal wanted to agree with her, but he was unsure that there would be enough people out there who would buy his brand of African-American fiction to the tune of him being able to quit his other job at the end of the semester.

The Kilgore Pickens project on the other hand possessed a bit more potential, at least in his mind. Still, who was he not to believe in himself on the issue of self-publishing if Yasmin did.

"I will do my absolute best," he said.

He didn't know exactly what that was, as his skill set up to that point had been confined to simply writing the books and promoting them (rather unsuccessfully). He tried to think of a world in which he excelled at all of the business-related elements of book publishing and wondered if that world could be the one he now occupied.

Why not?

KAMAL WAS RELUCTANT TO PART WITH YASMIN after they left the diner. He was still readjusting to being in her presence again and had yet to really determine what, if anything, had changed in how she felt about him. He still felt an overflowing of love toward her in his heart and assumed she was comfortable with all of this since he had already told her not once, but twice, that he loved her. Her reaction the second time signaled that there was a slight bit of evolution toward the idea of him feeling that way. Still, none of that signaled a change in her own feelings for him.

"Will I see you later tonight?" he asked, as they stood just outside the diner.

"I'll be gigging pretty late. I'll let you know how I'm feeling when we finish."

"Sure. Okay."

He escorted her back to her apartment and left so

that she could get some rest before she went to her Invisible People rehearsal. With time on his hands and nowhere to be for several hours, he decided to go hang out at one of the mega indoor newsstands in the midtown area.

City Periodicals and Papers carried quite a few magazines from all over the world and in more than twenty-five languages. One of the things he enjoyed most about the place is that it carried a wide variety of literary journals from across the country and from England and France. It was a way for him to keep up with what was being published in the world. Plus, he was always looking for new places to submit his shorter works. He believed it might have been his desire to gorge himself on literary fiction from around the world that made his African-American fiction a bit too far to the left. It wasn't that African-American readers, he believed, could not relate to other styles of fiction; it had more to do with the fact that publishers, in particular, believed that African-American readers only responded to a certain type of product—and apparently the product looked very little like what Kamal had been producing and was continuing to produce.

He picked up a few copies of the latest editions of his favorite literary magazines and headed to the subway. On the way home, he thumbed through a copy of *Granta*, one of the magazines he had picked up. He liked this one a lot, not just because of the great essays and short stories, but also because it had amazing photography and a nice sleek binding that made it nice to hold in his hands. He wondered, if things went well with the Kilgore Pickens project, if he might one day have one of his works accepted into the magazine. Kamal had decided that if he made any real money with Kilgore Pickens as his pseudonym that it made little sense for him to continue writing under the name Kamal Jackson. Why continue writing under a name that was kryptonite to publishers and was proving, very literally, to be worthless? He had no hesitation about leaping off of a sinking ship.

He wondered if thinking like that made him a sell out, the quintessential Uncle Tom. But then he thought about it: how can you sell out if you are not even selling? It was a conundrum he was willing to play to his advantage.

Even as he headed back to his apartment he considered the fact that he would not be able to carry through with a plan like that if he had been a singer like Yasmin. A singer could not disguise his or her voice normally. But of course there were always exceptions to the rule. One need look no further than the line of blue-eyed soul artists throughout the years. Even Bobby Caldwell's record label went so far as to disguise his whiteness for a while by putting out ambiguous record covers. Kamal guessed their thinking was that African Americans would not accept a classic like "What You Won't Do For Love" from someone whose melanin count was much lower. Of course, the label was wrong, but it didn't stop them from initiating a marketing plan that did just that.

Kamal was not a singer, though. He did his work on the page, and on the page, a person could become someone altogether different. Even before Kilgore Pickens, there was George Eliot. Even outside of women passing for men or African-American men passing for white men, there were white men passing for other white men. O. Henry. Mark Twain. And the list goes on and on. There was something about being able to transform oneself into something new, something magical. Kamal was just starting to feel the tingle that came along with such a sensation. He did not know why anyone, Yasmin included, would want to deny him the opportunity to experience that carefree luxury, but he knew the racial climate of the country was calling for African-American artists to unite behind a common African-American identity in the face of such hate, police brutality, and political neglect. Kamal could raise his fist in the air and yell out, "Power to the people!" Kilgore Pickens definitely could not.

When Kamal walked into his room, he lifted his phone to check for messages. Through all of the miscellaneous junk mail, there was one email, almost glimmering like the sun off of a Southern pond's rippling water.

Carson Matthews had responded!

## 20

Dear Mr. Pickens,

*Thank you for submitting your manuscript* Castle in the Field *for our consideration. After serious consideration, we have determined that your manuscript has a great deal of potential, and we would be interested in representing you.*

*For your convenience, we have attached our agency agreement to this email for your review. When would be a good time to talk to you, either in person or via phone? Please let us know your availability.*

*In the meantime, should you have any questions regarding either the agency agreement or the process of working with a literary agent, please do not hesitate to let us know by either email or by phone at (646) 555-1200.*

*Kindest regards,*

*Nelson Siblings*

*Carson Matthews Literary Agency*

After all of the effort Kamal had put into the Kilgore Pickens project, he had failed to consider that, at some point in the process, someone would actually want to talk to Kilgore Pickens. In person would have never happened, not for an agoraphobic writer like Kilgore Pickens. Still, there was a voice to create for an older white guy, and Kamal's voice, bred in Mississippi, honed in Atlanta, and polished in The City, was so far removed from that of an older white man's that he definitely needed a plan going forward on how to deal with the situation once and for all.

He already knew he would sign with the Carson Matthews Literary Agency; he just didn't know how to do that and maintain the kind of privacy necessary to see this plan all the way through to the end. Was Nelson Siblings or Carson Matthews even trustworthy enough to handle the truth going forward. Would they still be interested in him if he told the truth? Just how far could he get before someone figured him out. You really could not trust anyone these days. J.K. Rowling had only had her pseudonymous novel out a few months before someone dimed her out. If you could not keep the name of a billionaire secret, Kamal did not think the odds were in his favor.

He thought about trying to disguise his voice, but he was not a voice actor and doubted he could sustain the same artificial voice over time. He might have been good for a few weeks, or even a few months, but what would happen when, down the road, he called the agency and his voice did something different? That would be the first crack in his façade. From there, it would roll downhill very quickly.

Another option was to have his roommate, James, do the voice. That was not an entirely bad idea either, considering that James was a trained and employed actor and would probably pull it off rather convincingly. But for however many years this thing could potentially last? That was just kicking the same ball a little farther down the road. Plus, he was unsure if he would even be living with James years from now. There were just too many variables in that plan that he couldn't possibly account for. So with a pang of regret, Kamal casted that idea to the side as well.

For the rest of the afternoon, he brainstormed ideas, nothing sticking. There were a million things threatening his plan before he even got it out the gate. Finally, as the clock approached five, he decided to take a break and grab a bite to eat. His composition class that evening started in two hours, and he had to look over his lesson plan once more before going to work. That night they would be working on comparison and contrast essays. While he could have easily taught the class from memory, after several years of having taught it already, he still believed in going into the room as sharp as possible. Plus, while the textbooks only changed in the slowest of evolutionary ways, mainly through the examples employed throughout the book, Kamal was constantly seeking new ways to keep his pedagogy fresh and interesting. Each year he got a bit older, and each year his students got a bit younger (although there were also a nice number of nontraditional students to round out the discussions). With an ever-changing student make-up, he had to constantly refine his approach to the subject matter. One of the things he added this semester in both sections of his English composition class was more music-related topics to write about. This was largely due to Kamal's being inspired by Yasmin. In fact, the comparison and contrast essay they had to work on that evening called for the class to compare and contrast Kendrick Lamar's *To Pimp A Butterfly* album to Marvin Gaye's *What's Going On* album. The common denominator, Kamal felt, was that each was a type of protest album, but where else did the similarities exist? What were the strongest differences there as well? Ironically, the younger people in the class were not attracted to writing about Marvin

Gaye, and the older students were not interested in writing about Kendrick Lamar. The beauty of the assignment, though, was that it forced both groups of students to step outside of their comfort zones and try something new.

Kamal gathered his materials together for class and placed them in his messenger bag. He then tossed on his teaching uniform: a pair of khakis and a button-up shirt. As he left the apartment, he tried to pull his mind away from the Kilgore Pickens dilemma. Surely the answer would come to him soon, he hoped, locking the door behind himself.

After his class ended, Kamal headed over to the bookstore down the street from the college. He often went there to grab a smoothie and decompress. Occasionally, he made notes on a story he was working on or read one of the weekly news magazines.

He ordered his smoothie, then took a seat at a small table near the cafe window. He normally people-watched on evenings like this. The view was always great. As his eyes followed a group of Japanese tourists up the street, he overheard a kid asking his mother for a book. The kid had to have been around ten years old. The book the kid was holding up to his mother was one of Lemony Snicket's *A Series of Unfortunate Events* books.

Then it struck Kamal like a lightning bolt being hurled through the heavens by Zeus himself what he needed to do. Before Daniel Handler became widely known as Lemony Snicket, he had played the part of Lemony Snicket's "handler," and apt word, if ever there were one. Because Lemony Snicket did not talk to the public, he allegedly communicated through Daniel Handler (the actual author). It hardly took a second to realize Daniel Handler and Lemony Snicket were one in the same. (After all, Lemony Snicker rhymed with Jiminy Cricket, making it nearly impossible to believe the name as anything other than an odd pseudonym that rhymed with a famous Disney character.) That's what Kamal would do. He would pass off his best version of *Finding Forester*, the Gus Van Zant film about an older white male writer who was a recluse and how he made friends with a talented and upcoming basketball player-slash-writer who was an African-American high school student, recently admitted to one of the best academies in the city (coincidentally the alma mater of the white writer). The film posed an interesting question: could the next J.D. Salinger or whoever be in the form of a black kid who wore baggy pants and had a better grasp of the English language than his teachers? The movie was entertaining, in spite of the complexities of its racial dynamics. Why could there not be an older white man who had a college-educated African-American guy as his "helper"? In the racial climate of America, Kamal knew there would be a lot of people willing to believe he was just "the help." So why not play that assumption against them?

It was then that he decided he would be Kilgore Pickens's handler. It was not unlike what William Faulkner had written in "A Rose for Emily," Kamal figured: It was the kind of lie only an obtuse white man could believe. Kamal did not think that was necessarily Carson Matthews or his minions, but at the same time, he did not think they would guess any differently, because decades of African-American sidekicks and media portrayals of African Americans as anything but scholars had conditioned most white people to be accepting of the scenario Kamal was proposing. It would not seem odd at all. In fact, it would seem (and feel) natural.

It was only when Kamal came to that conclusion that he responded to the email (in Kilgore's voice, using the new Gmail account he had created) and informed them that they would be talking directly with his assistant, Mr. Kamal Jackson.

---

KAMAL RESPONDED TO NELSON SIBLINGS EMAIL minutes before Yasmin arrived. He was pumped and excited and wanted to tell her all of the good news about what was happening. He wanted to let her know for the first time in his writing career he would not have the proverbial racial ceiling over his head. He would write about whatever he wanted to write about. He could have his work exist in its own space and people reading it without regard to what he looked like or what race he was. While he knew signing with a literary agent did not automatically mean that he would get a book deal, he reasoned that it was virtually impossible for an editor at a major publishing house to ignore a client of the Carson Matthews Literary Agency. Those editors might very well second-guess themselves before they second-guessed Carson Matthews. He was one of their best chances at having an author bring home a major award, whether it be a Pulitzer, National Book Award, or even a MacArthur Genius fellowship. Signing with Carson Matthews was the closest thing to a slam dunk in an industry where people largely took outside shots. Still, Kamal was unsure of how Yasmin would react to the deception at the heart of his great news.

He decided to hold off on telling her until he could

figure out a way to do it where she did not make him feel like a mustache-twisting, race-betraying villain. He knew she would sense his added enthusiasm in their love making, but he did not dare tell her the sensation stemmed from more than being enveloped once again between her soft, voluptuous thighs.

That night he climaxed just shy of the infamous "petit mort." He had not yet allowed himself to accept the thought that great sex could cause one to lose consciousness, but it was nice to reach a point where you became dizzy with ecstasy. He had heard of people blacking out during sex, and he wondered if that would ever happen to him. After a while, he thought it impossible for himself in particular, in the same way that some people pass out at the sight of blood or a baby being born through natural delivery, but he did not.

He also didn't think he would want to see Yasmin pass out either. Seeing her unconscious in his bed would not make him assume that she had succumbed to petit mort's erotic abyss; on the contrary, he would probably fear that she had a far more serious medical condition. He would have called an ambulance for her and been seated at her side in City Memorial Hospital before a doctor revealed that she had just been overstimulated during sex and simply passed out.

He knew his ideas were ridiculous, but as he lay beside her, his body still buzzing from the orgasm that felt like it was radiating out of every pore in his body, he could not stop his mind from considering the possibilities.

When Kamal was finally able to steel his thoughts, he began to think about what lay ahead. He had to be able to approach each of these upcoming things with a degree of confidence he had not yet expressed in any of his other endeavors. In order for him to do that, he couldn't concern himself with obstacles like whether or not Yasmin would co-sign on his work. All that was important, as far as their relationship was concerned, was that they continued to anchor themselves emotionally and physically in each other.

Or so he thought.

"So I see that you are a writer, as well, Mr. Jackson," said Nelson Siblings over the phone. His voice was very quiet, yet pointed, the kind of voice that was like a pebble: deceptive in size, but still capable of sinking to the bottom of the ocean.

"Yes, I write and teach, when I am not handling the affairs of Mr. Pickens."

"Clearly, we would prefer to talk directly to Mr. Pickens, but since that's not possible, we'll do our best to work with you on making sure we're able to have the best version of the manuscript reach the best publisher."

"I understand—and I am sure Mr. Pickens appreciates this," Kamal responded.

He had gone online and done some research about what constituted a legitimate power of attorney document for the state and cobbled one together, adding all of the relevant signatures himself. The document was fake, and he wondered what would happen to him if the document he created was ever discovered as being fake. The thought scared him a bit, and he opted, instead, to play a heavier roll in being the handler, which

Kamal saw as a person who merely assisted, but did not do actually do the core work of the individual. Legally, he could not have power of attorney over a fictitious person, he assumed, but it might still give him room to allow Kilgore Pickens to sign documents and other materials without there needing to be a legally binding element tying Kamal to anything. So he sent a letter from Kilgore Pickens, who then spoke of his agoraphobia and desire to not be a public individual, and asked that any correspondence be done through Kamal Jackson and that Kilgore Pickens would be the one making the decisions and authorizing the various elements of the negotiating, as well as the final deal.

"Well, Mr. Jackson, I am in the process of putting together a few notes, most of them dealing with suggestions on the pace of the second half of the book. I will get those to you by the end of this week, and you can then pass them along to Mr. Pickens."

"Sure. No problem."

Once they got off the phone, Kamal thought about the second half of the book and realized that was the part that largely went unchanged from the original *The Princess of Fall* manuscript. In his haste to get the project underway, he had only changed the first half of the book around to look drastically different—and this was mainly to throw off editorial assistants who had read only the first few chapters of the book before rejecting it when he submitted it under his real name. He'd assumed that would be enough. Thankfully, though, it seemed Nelson Siblings wanted him to alter the second half of the book, as well, thereby giving him what amounted to a far more different (in appearance) look than the most original version of the manuscript. In essence, doing this write over would protect his ass much more than having just redone the first half.

Kamal opened his laptop, and began isolating the second half of the book in his writing software so that he could make changes, line by line and chapter by chapter.

Not wanting to jump too far ahead of himself, though, he decided to reread the second half of the book and keep an open mind for the notes that Nelson would send later in the week.

———

KAMAL GOT THE NOTES BY THE END OF THE WEEK, made the corrections, and sent them back to Nelson Siblings. He took his time responding, though. He didn't want Kilgore Pickens to seem like he was a fast writer. Kamal had only planned to write one book under this pseudonym for now. If things went well, he would consider doing one every few years, maybe even spacing out the novels ten years at a time, since there were several authors who had made a thing of spacing out their books by nearly a decade or more.

To deal with the advance that would likely come as soon as the novel sold, Kamal chatted up a classmate from Ellison-Wright College who had become an attorney in Mississippi. The recommendation was that Kamal start an LLC entitled KP Literary, LLC, and make himself the managing member of the LLC. The LLC would, in reality, be a single member LLC, but most people wouldn't know what to make of that designation anyway, except for maybe an accountant or member of the IRS. All of the copyrights would then be assigned to this business entity by Kamal. Because publishing companies tended to handle the copyright registrations of manuscripts they were publishing on their own, it would be a bizarre and seemingly amateurish move to negotiate with Nelson Siblings about letting Kilgore Pickens copyright his own work ahead of time. The reason for this awkward gesture was that it would ultimately force anyone going forward, publisher included, to negotiate with KP Literary as the actual holder of the copyright, not Kilgore Pickens directly. Also, it would allow Kamal the opportunity to sign any agreements on behalf of Kilgore Pickens, acting as the designated manager of the KP Literary Limited Liability Company.

When Kamal's classmate first told him how all of this worked, Kamal thought it would be too thin a veil to fool anyone. "You're a young black man, and he is an old white man. People would have no problem thinking of you as his assistant. Just don't correct them."

The reason for the copyright registration move was to prevent the appearance of anything fraudulent, meaning that a fake person could not assign a copyright he did not hold, and Kamal would be exposed immediately—and so would go the entire operation.

It didn't take Nelson Siblings a month to stimulate enough interest in the recently discovered Mississippi-born author, heir apparent to the likes of William Faulkner and Eudora Welty, to generate enough interest to get an auction going among three different publishing houses, all of them major houses. Nelson confided in Kamal that he thought Kilgore Pickens's peculiar ways and his reluctance to go public gave him an air of mystery that tickled the imaginations of publishers looking for the next Salinger or Pynchon. When Kamal heard this over the phone, he allowed a huge smile to spread across his face.

As the auction went on, Kamal allowed himself to consider what his project had actually revealed to him about the publishing industry. The core of the story he had submitted to Nelson Siblings was the same that had been shot down when he was a client of Vanessa Travont. She had all but kicked him out of her office that Sunday morning, telling him that no publisher wanted his book, and that as an African-American writer, he had to do a much better job of considering his market. What did it now mean that the exact same core idea was being so readily embraced by the larger publishing industry now that his ethnicity was no longer directly attached to the project? To call the industry racist would be an overstatement, in the same way to call it sexist would be an overstatement. It could easily be that there were enough flawed individuals in the general population that it was inevitable that a number of them would show up in the publishing sector and ultimately impact how many of the publishing houses acted. Kamal was not being critical; he was just doing what was necessary to get a fair shake in light of this reality.

After several days, the auction concluded, and Kamal received a call from Nelson.

"Kamal, I know that Kilgore does not take phone calls, but you have to allow me to speak to him this one time and tell him the good news!" Nelson Siblings gushed.

"I wish I could do that, Nelson. You know I do. But Kilgore is really OCD about things. He wants things done a very particular way or else he becomes very difficult to deal with. Whatever you tell me, you know you can count on me to deliver it with the same enthusiasm as you."

Nelson paused. "Well, you know, it was worth a try, right?"

Kamal chuckled lightly under his breath. "Yeah. So

what is the result of the auction?"

"We got him a good deal! A really good deal!"

"How good?"

"Six hundred thousand dollars!"

Kamal jumped out of his chair and began dancing around the room. He couldn't remember being this elated about anything since President Obama got elected in November of 2008. He did all of this in near silence.

Not skipping a beat, he responded as calmly as he could muster, "That's wonderful news! I'll let him know as soon as you and I hang up. May I ask who won the auction?"

"Polar Bear, U.S.A.! They will deliver the first two hundred thousand dollars once the contract is signed, the second two hundred thousand dollars when the final manuscript is approved, and the final two hundred thousand at publication."

"I will definitely let him know. Thank you so much, Nelson. Feel free to forward the paperwork to the P.O. Box I emailed you earlier. We will get them back to you as soon as we can."

"Sure thing," Nelson responded. "Are you sure you don't want me to just messenger the paperwork over right now? From your cell phone number, I'm guessing you two might actually be in The City. You can give me an address and..."

Kamal sighed, still awed by Nelson's persistence on meeting someone he would never meet. "He's going to want you to mail it. He's a patient man." Then Kamal added, "Much more patient than I am."

"Me, too," Nelson replied, chuckling.

When Kamal got off the phone, he screamed as loudly as he could, pumping the air. "Yes! Yes! Yes!" Again, he started to dance. He was so caught up in his dancing that he did not notice James standing in the doorway.

"Is everything all right? I heard you carrying on in here," James said.

"I just got some really amazing news," Kamal responded, silently kicking himself for drawing so much attention to himself.

James walked into his room and sat down on the foot of the bed. "So what's the great news, roomie?" James's face lit up, clearly happy for whatever Kamal was now experiencing.

Kamal almost told him everything right then and there, but he found his bearings and responded awkwardly, "I can't really say. It's kind of confidential."

"Are you serious?" James said. "I didn't realize we had secrets."

"You know it's not like that. I'm just not allowed to tell anybody yet. I have been told to keep everything under wraps for now."

"Well, can I at least get a hint?"

Kamal smiled. "I can't do that."

"What if I guess it? Can you just nod or blink your eyes or something?"

"James, come on, man. I can't say a word."

"You got a book deal for your novella?"

Kamal had actually forgotten about the novella. It had been selling very slowly on Amazon, and he had totally ignored it in favor of what was happening with his Kilgore Pickens Project.

"I can't say," he finally responded.

"Okay. Well, I'll leave you alone then," James said, turning to leave. "I'll just ask Yasmin later." He winked and smiled and headed out of the room.

Yasmin, Kamal thought. Oh shit. Would he be able to hide something this huge from her?

He would find out soon enough when she came over later that evening. Until then, he closed his door, and continued dancing.

23

When Yasmin came over later that night, Kamal had her sit on the end of the bed, while he sat in his writer's chair facing her.

"I have to tell you something, and I need you to hear me out first," he started.

"Okay."

At that moment he wondered if she actually loved him. If she did, might she have responded a bit more anxiously? She appeared as though this was just another conversation in a long line of conversations, and his needing to preference the conversation at all had no bearing whatsoever on how she might react.

He continued. "Do you remember that novel I wrote a while back called *The Princess of Fall*?"

"The one you started changing. Yeah, I remember it. Did you decide to finish it?"

Still, her reactions were nonchalant. Her mind was clearly in another space or maybe another place. Maybe this conversation was getting in the way of their intimacy. If that were the case, then nothing had changed from the night of their first major fight; they had only grown to accept the other's position a bit better.

"Yes and yes," he responded. "I finished it, and I submitted it to a few literary agents under a pseudonym. One picked it up."

"Pseudonym?"

"Yeah, I used a fake name when I submitted it."

"What name did you use?" she asked.

Kamal had expected for this part of the conversation to be overshadowed by the joy of her learning that a literary agent had attached himself to the project. He was wrong.

"Kilgore Pickens."

"Kilgore Pickens? What kind of name is that?"

"About as far away as you can get from Kamal Jackson."

Yasmin nibbled on her lower lip. "I see."

"Well, I submitted to a few of the top literary agents in The City, and I heard back from a few. In fact, I signed with the biggest and most prestigious agency in The City."

"Wow," she deadpanned.

"I know. And they were able to get a deal with a big publisher today. Polar Bear! And guess how much the deal is for?" he said, his enthusiasm blocking out all of the blasé reaction she was giving him.

"How much?" she responded. "Just how much are you being paid to sell out? I'm curious. Inquiring minds want to know."

Kamal snapped out of his buzz immediately, completely sober. This is what he had feared when he thought about coming to her with this. There was a part of him that was relieved, though. At least she knew the truth of what he had been doing now, and he didn't have to sneak around acting like none of this was going on. Still, he didn't like the look in her eyes. It was as if he had completely disappointed her, abandoned her trust, abandoned his people. Could he really do all of those things by simply writing a book and using a different name?

"All right," he responded, exasperated, realizing that it didn't matter whether he had signed a deal for one thousand dollars or for one million dollars. Her reaction would have been the same. "I know you don't care for what I did—and I respect that—but as your friend, I was hoping that you would at least be understanding, if not even supporting of what's going on in my life."

Yasmin looked up at the ceiling for a moment, as if considering his words, albeit reluctantly. "So," she finally started, "with all of the things going on in America, you're deciding to 'pass' and write white? All of these young black men being murdered by police officers, black women dying under mysterious circumstances while in police custody—not to mention the rapes, all of these things plaguing our community, all of these things that you, as a writer, have the opportunity to address and bring voice to are being set to the side, all in the name of profit? You know what I loved about your writing?"

It was the first time she had really used the word "love" in any manner in connection with him, but the way in which she did it felt painful to hear. Although the question was designed to be rhetorical, Kamal still felt compelled to answer, "What?"

"You were true to who you were. You might not have written the most popular style of fiction out there, but you were writing stories that were true to who you are as a person. There's a pocket of people out there who appreciate that, whether the publishers do or don't. I still think you could have done your own thing as a self-published author and built your audience slowly. We're out there. We just might not have been aware of your work yet. I'm fortunate in that I did hear about it—and I have told everyone I could tell about it, too." She sighed and shook her head. "I just feel like you're only doing this because you feel unappreciated. I can't control how you feel, but I can tell that you're definitely appreciated."

Kamal nodded his understanding. "Well, thanks for sharing that with me."

"Without that level of commitment to who you are, I have to admit, I'm a bit turned off by you."

"What?"

"Your willingness to do your own thing was a sexy quality to me. I'm not saying that I'm not physically attracted to you or anything—because I am—but you go from being just another fine brother to being on a Tyson Beckford kind of level with it, simply based off the swag you have from your originality."

"So you're saying that because I decided to publish under a pseudonym and cater primarily to a white audience, I'm someone you wouldn't want to fuck with?" Kamal asked, a bit taken aback.

Yasmin shrugged her shoulders. "I'm just not feeling this vibe right now."

Kamal leaned toward her and attempted to kiss her and bring her back down to the reality he felt she needed to be in, but she turned her face away from him and he caught only her cheek.

"Wow," he said, his voice flat with the realization that she was giving him an ultimatum. "So if I give up this deal, we can be together, but if I keep it, then we're finished?"

Yasmin reached for each of his hands and placed them in hers. "Kamal, I know I've given you some grief about the nature of our relationship in the past and whether or not we should talk about loving each other. I believe that there's a part of me that wants so desperately to love you, but there's another part of me that fears getting hurt. If we were to stay together, I think I would grow out of that at some point, although, truthfully, it hasn't happened yet. What I can tell you for sure is this: if you want to go around masquerading as some white dude to sell books when we need people like you serving as the griots for our community, then I'm not feeling that about you, and it makes me not want to be around a person who would do that."

"So I can't do both? You know, I still have that novella."

"The fact that you're getting paid to do this and neutering your own work to get it through, I can only look at that. When I see you, that's what I will think about."

Kamal's brow furrowed. "So you wouldn't think about us making love or spending time together?"

Yasmin shrugged her shoulders. "I don't really know. I just know right now that I'm thinking about this situation you just told me about." And then she added, "And I don't think of what we do as making love."

"What do you see it as then?" he asked.

"Having sex."

"That's it? That's all there is between us? After all this time?"

"What else could it be? I am not ready to use the word 'love' to describe how I feel about you."

Kamal knew he should have been prepared to hear her say those words, but there was a part of him that thrived off of hope, the hope that their reconnecting had somehow moved the needle on her emotions. He had invested himself in the idea that that was the case.

He now knew that nothing had really changed. He didn't want to give up six hundred thousand dollars in the hope of something happening that might never happen, and he decided to let Yasmin know as much.

"I'm going to do this book deal."

This time Yasmin leaned over and kissed him tenderly on the lips. "Okay, boo. You do you. I'll do me. It was real while it lasted."

And with that, she rose from the bed and walked out of the room and out of the apartment.

This time, as Kamal sat in his writing chair, he knew that it was officially over.

## 24

## ELEVEN MONTHS LATER

The fact that *Castle in the Field* (formerly known as *The Princess of Fall*) was published eleven months from the date of the signing of the contract was a minor miracle, as far as Kamal was concerned. His other two novels had taken much closer to eighteen months to be published. He didn't know whether the buzz around the auction had escalated the release date and placed him directly into the Christmas season or if it was because he had previously been on a release schedule for the quintessential and underrated African-American writer.

Even though he had already been paid the first two installments of his advance, minus his agency percentage of fifteen percent, as well as the foreign rights that he was fortunate enough to sell ahead of the book's domestic release, thereby pocketing him a nice bit of extra change in his pockets, he had not yet moved out of his apartment with James. He didn't know if it was because he was trying desperately to keep all of this a secret or if he just preferred the life he had developed for himself ever since he had first moved to The City. There was, however, an innate fear that someone would figure him out at some point in time.

And if they did, he did not know if it was legally possible for Polar Bear to come to him requesting their advance money back, so the six hundred thousand plus dollars felt almost like ill-gotten loot that he would forfeit at some point in the future.

Kamal didn't know what to do if the book sales took off and he ended up making back the advance and then eventually earning royalties on top of that. Even more, he had declined to do any interviews that were not in writing and only from the higher tier periodicals. Even at his own admission, Kamal had poured it on so unnecessarily thick that no one seemed to notice that he would have settled for much less in the way of publicity. The biggest issue, as far as the press was concerned, however, was that they wanted to get a picture of the author. Untold numbers of fact checking departments had committed themselves to the task of trying to track down a photograph of Kilgore Pickens, and while they did come across people with that same name, none of them confessed to being the writer in question.

The vigilance with which the periodicals pursued information about Kilgore Pickens actually scared Kamal a bit, making him even more skeptical about spending much of the money he had acquired through the book deal.

A week before the book was released, there was a write up in The City Review, an insert in The City Times that was released on the first Sunday of the month, the issue that those in the literary world clamored to read, as it represented the creme of the creme in an arena where everyone was constantly vying for the higher rungs of the literary ladder. Kilgore had landed a front page, above the fold, article of around a thousand words, and since there was no picture of the author available, they had a picture of a white woman reading his book. The picture, to Kamal, said a thousand words. Not only was it sanctioned by white readers; it was also being positioned as an excellent Christmas gift.

Things were going well, and Kamal couldn't walk in front of a bookstore that didn't have the book sitting in the window with a larger poster of the cover floating nearby. Even African-American bookstores had copies of the book sitting in highly visible spaces in their stores, although there, in theory, weren't any African-American characters anywhere in the story. It was safe to say that Kilgore Pickens was the hottest author going, and there were even rumblings, according to Nelson Siblings, that the book might be in the running for several different awards.

It was a dream come true for any writer, but Kamal found himself too nervous to talk about it to anyone. It was a secret that he held with one other person—who had decided not to deal with him in any way going forward.

At times, Kamal lay in his bed, looking up at the ceiling, worried. He wondered if Yasmin, in an act of defiance and retribution, would reveal to the world that he was Kilgore Pickens. If she did in fact do that, then what would be the backlash?

The book was the book, after all. If people liked the book, they simply liked the book. Who wrote the book should have been largely irrelevant. He felt the same way about the Milli Vanilli situation, too. For the people who cried foul because the two lead singers had lip synced their performances, they failed to realize something, Kamal reasoned. The voices on the song *were* the voices on the song. In other words, musically speaking, no one was duped from an audio perspective.

As a matter of marketing and visuals (or optics, as millennial marketers liked to say), the façade of the group fell apart in the public eye and forced the singers to give back their Grammy awards and the record companies to reimburse certain fans for the money they paid for the album in the first place. In 2015, was it still possible that something like that could happen—even to a writer?

Kilgore Pickens never said he was white, nor did Kamal. He assumed that, just like many white readers, the larger public would make the assumption that he was white. Hell, even in Kamal's mind, he had envisioned Kilgore Pickens as an older white man. It would have been difficult to plant an African-American man into the shoes of someone with Kilgore Pickens's background, especially being from Mississippi. Still, if Kamal needed to fall back on something for the sake of some protection, he could fake like Kilgore Pickens was never supposed to be taken as a white writer. It was a fragile assertion, but an assertion nonetheless.

There were days when Kamal was happy about the success of the book, but on most days the sells of the book only served to make him feel more uncomfortable. When the first journalist wrote about his enigmatic nature in an article entitled "Who is Kilgore Pickens?", he felt for sure that he was done. The article regurgitated the bio that Polar Bear had given in the publicity releases, but it went one step further: the article concluded with the assumption that Kilgore Pickens was the pseudonym for a famous popular fiction writer.

Kamal figured at some point the idea of a pseudonym would likely fall onto the table, but he had hoped it would take much longer for that to happen.

He just didn't want his own name to come up in the discussion.

As industry speculation continued, Kamal worried that, at minimum, Nelson Siblings would put two and two together, but that not had not happened. Nelson was committed to the idea that Kamal was "the help" and there was no amount of prodding that would get him to relinquish that idea and consider another, more plausible possibility.

Rumors abounded that Kilgore Pickens was really Philip Roth, an internationally acclaimed Jewish novelist whose name had perpetually come up over and over in discussions surrounding the Nobel Prize for Literature. Because Philip Roth had talked publicly about retiring from novel writing for years, content to let his canon speak for itself, many conspiracy theorists began to suspect that this was Philip Roth's way of returning to the industry, much in the way that J.K. Rowling had done after the publication of *A Casual Vacancy*, when she switched to writing mysteries under the male pen name Robert Galbraith.

When Kamal learned of this particular theory, a smile spread across his face. There was no way in the world people would suspect him as the real writer of Kilgore Pickens's book if names as heavy-hitting as Philip Roth's were floating around and being taken seriously. It was almost flattering to hear the things these conspiracy theorists came up with.

Kamal would have been happy to just sit back and let whatever unfold and collect his checks on his recently celebrated best seller, but a single phone call would disrupt all of that.

"May I speak to Mr. Kamal Jackson?" a nasally voice said. The man sounded as if he were an early twenty-something white male, the articulation in his voice a bit too formal.

"This is he," Kamal responded.

"My name is Tucker Beaumont, and I work with *The City Press*. Is it okay if I ask you a few questions?"

"*The City Press*? Wow. To what do I owe this call."

"You a reader of *The City Press*?"

"Always have been," Kamal responded. "It's the only real paper for true artists and people who don't really give a damn about crossword puzzles."

Tucker laughed, relaxing a bit—which is what Kamal had intended—before saying, "I just have a few questions for you?"

"What about?"

"I wanted to talk with you about Kilgore Pickens."

It must be about his being Kilgore's handler, he thought. "Sure."

"I'm doing a story about plagiarism, and I was fortunate enough to come across a copy of a manuscript you submitted to Spectrum Press entitled *The Princess of Fall*. I was informed by their editor that they were on the verge of accepting the manuscript when they noticed that Kilgore Pickens had written a very similar story called *Castle in the Field*."

Damn! Kamal thought, cursing himself. He had assumed after his first few rejections that he would not ever hear from the remaining independent publishers to whom he had submitted. It was a calculated risk, he knew, when he proceeded with the Kilgore Pickens project, but one he felt confident in taking at the time. He had apparently miscalculated horribly.

Not knowing what to do, Kamal responded, "I have no idea what you're talking about." He knew as soon as the words left his lips that he had only insulted the intelligence of the person on the other end of the phone, and that would ultimately not bode well for him.

"You don't know what I'm talking about?" Tucker Beaumont repeated. "Well, let me help you. After reviewing both manuscripts, side by side, I noticed that there were some changes throughout the book, particularly the first half, but there was no question that it was the same story. So that leaves me with one of two conclusions: (1) you clearly plagiarized a bestselling author, one that no one has ever laid eyes on in life, except for you, or (2) you are in fact Mr. Pickens, and you rewrote the manuscript because you thought it might be better received under a pseudonym. Now, you could either tell me which one it is, or you will leave me with little choice but to write my story using my own assumption."

"If you do, then I will sue you for libel," Kamal said. He tried to make his voice sound firm, but he was terribly uncomfortable and entirely outside of his league.

"Mr. Jackson, it's in your best interest to talk to me

about this. The story I write will help to shape the discussion on this. Just think about it. If I could piece the facts of this story together—a*nd I write for a free weekly paper*—imagine what would happen if the spotlight team at a rag like *The City Times* got ahold of this story. I'm willing to bet that they would not be nearly as kind as I would."

"Hold on for a second," Kamal said, placing the phone on mute and pacing his room. He had too many thoughts running through his head at the moment. Of course, he could keep denying, but the bottom line was that he was going to make the news regardless of if he wanted to or not. He considered calling Nelson Siblings and breaking the news to him directly first, but the idea of telling Nelson that he had lied to him for roughly a year was too nerve-wracking to indulge in at the moment. Maybe Tucker Beaumont could help him spin the story if he decided to do the interview. Anything to soften the blow. Maybe he could come clean once and for all and let the world know about the reasons he had to do it. It was all too much to process. Finally, Kamal unmuted the telephone and said, "Why don't we meet up a the Starbucks on 11th and 8th tomorrow morning at 9:00 a.m., and I will be happy to answer whatever questions you might have."

"9:00? I can do that. Do me a favor, though, and don't talk to anyone until after we have had a chance to talk."

"Sure thing. I don't have any interest in talking to anyone else. But I would like you to keep a lid on things, as well. Meet me in the morning, and I will tell you everything you need to know."

"All right. Well, I'll see you then."

Kamal hung up his phone and fell face-first onto

his bed. The world seemed to be spinning around him, as he could feel his body sinking further and further into the comforter. This was how it would end, he thought, before closing his eyes and trying to tune out the world for a few hours.

———

BY THE TIME KAMAL WOKE UP THE FOLLOWING morning, his name had been splashed across social media as the writer behind the infamous Kilgore Pickens. At first Kamal had assumed Tucker Beaumont had reneged on his promise not to run the story, but after combing through the various hashtags throughout Twitter, it became clear that someone at Spectrum Press had leaked it online, and people quickly jumped all over it, pressing it to the top of the trending topics list.

Before he was able to tie his shoes so he could leave the apartment, James appeared in his doorway.

"So you were the person who wrote that book everyone's talking about?"

"Yeah."

"You should have told me, man."

"I know. Hey, I'm sorry. Everything was happening so fast, and I was hoping no one would ever know."

James said nothing for a moment, just looked at Kamal. "I just want to know one thing."

"What's that?"

"Why did you do it?"

Kamal took a deep breath. "I felt it was the only way anyone would take me seriously as a writer."

James nodded his head slowly. "I see."

He turned around slowly and walked away.

Kamal sat on the edge of the bed, one shoe tied,

the other one loose. He had an hour to get to the coffee shop to meet Tucker Beaumont, and he knew the entire trip there would be one of the slowest, most difficult trips to his inevitable date with the literary guillotine.

When Kamal walked into Starbucks, he immediately found Tucker Beaumont (whose image he had googled) sitting in the back of the room, a perturbed look on his red face. Kamal figured that Tucker would not be very happy that the Internet got the jump on the story about Kilgore Pickens, so Kamal pondered ways to make it up to him on the way over—if only, because he knew he needed someone who had access to a barrel of ink to spin this entire mess for him.

"Hi, Tucker," he said, extending his hand.

"If it isn't *the* Kamal Jackson," Tucker responded, unable to conceal his sarcasm.

"Hey, listen, man. I know you're upset about everything getting out on the Internet, but I was hoping that I could right things by giving you an exclusive."

Tucker sighed. "You were already going to do that. Unless you are going to tell me something that the world doesn't already know, then I don't see what there is to gain at this point."

Kamal considered this for a moment. "I can give you the 'why' part. Up till now, everything is just speculation. You can really define the story in a way that does away with the speculation."

"And you are willing to go on record with all of this?"

"Yes."

Tucker smiled, an act that Kamal did not readily expect to see. "Well, I know the perfect place for us to talk."

GILLIAM COLLEGE WAS ONLY FIVE BLOCKS AWAY from Starbucks, and Tucker had already reserved a research carrel on one of the upper floors of the college library. The room was only accessible by a key, and other than the head librarian, no one else had a key to that particular room, Tucker informed him.

Tucker patiently pulled out his notebook and took his cell phone and positioned it between him and Kamal.

"Tell me a little about how you became a writer," Tucker said.

"Well, I started writing stories and poems back in middle school, but I didn't get serious about it until my second year as an English major at Ellison Wright College."

"Where is Ellison Wright? I haven't heard of that one."

"It's a historically black college in southwest Atlanta. It's responsible for the largest number of African Americans admitted to law schools," Kamal said, trying to ignore the condescending tone Tucker used.

"Good to know. I see you got your first book published a little over four years ago. Tell me about that experience," Tucker said.

"Well, I wrote the novel while working at a book-store after I graduated from college. I didn't really know what to do with it, so I started writing short stories. One of them got picked up by an anthology, and the agent who represented the editor of that anthology eventually became my agent."

Tucker nodded. "I see your last book came out as a paperback original a little over a year ago. That's pretty recent. Frankly, I am surprised you're not still touring off that book."

"Sales have been a little slow," Kamal responded. He started to tell Tucker that the only way you could get one of his books was to go to Nell's bookstore up-town. Elsewhere in The City, a potential reader would have to visit the kiosk and place an order to have it shipped to his house—that, or simply order it from Amazon.

Tucker jotted this among the notes he had been taking. "So did this slowing down of sales affect your decision to publish under a pseudonym?"

Kamal thought the question a very obvious one, but he still answered as if it were equally as valid as the rest purported to be. "Yes."

Tucker leaned in closely now. He even moved the microphone a little closer to Kamal. "So, tell me, Ka-mal, how did you come up with the idea for Kilgore Pickens?"

This was it. This was where he would tell the story and completely unburdened himself of the weight he had been carrying. For some reason, Paul Laurence Dunbar's poem "We Wear the Mask," a poem about how African Americans must often conceal their true selves in America in order to fit in, came to mind. This would be the moment Kamal took off the mask. He didn't know if Tucker Beaumont was the best person for him to reveal himself to, but he realized Tucker was likely the lesser of the evils that awaited him.

"My agent, Vanessa Travont, dropped me after Stalling Press passed on the book that would become *Castle in the Field*. I think she tired of me writing work that had very little commercial viability and decided to cut her losses. I was told by nearly everyone that my work didn't appeal to most African-American readers. Somehow my work was *too white*. So, first I tried to shop my novel to smaller, independent publishers, and when the rejections started mounting, I got the idea to resubmit it under a pseudonym," Kamal said.

"But why an older white male?" Tucker asked.

"You're the one who said that he's white. I never explicitly led anyone to believe anything about his ethnicity."

"You described him as white in his bio, the one circulating around with the press release," Tucker said.

"Actually, no. But your assumption is part of the problem I hoped to address by using a name like Kilgore Pickens and giving a background like I did. In the absence of ethnic signifiers, white readers assume that a character or a person is white. It's as if every person of color is obligated to announce his or her ethnicity every time they introduce a character. It's a pretty silly double standard.

"I read somewhere that the cool thing about judo, as a martial art form, is that it requires the user to find ways of using his opponent's weight and momentum against himself. This is the same principle. I just left enough space for people to draw whatever conclusions they wanted to draw," Kamal responded. He felt it unnecessary to talk about how he deliberately set out to create a white persona. He preferred this version of the truth much better for publicity purposes.

"You had to know that the public was reacting to Kilgore Pickens as a white male writer in the vein of Faulkner and Updike, though, right?" Tucker said.

Kamal nodded. "I admire those writers. It's always nice to be compared to them."

"And the Philip Roth rumors? I'm sure you heard those, as well. You could have stopped them at any point. Why didn't you?"

"I didn't feel it was my responsibility to address rumors."

"Okay," Tucker responded. "Well, since this is the angle you're going to take, I must confess that I spoke to your agent, Nelson Siblings, and he talked about the elaborate lengths you went through to protect your identity from even them. Why would you not at least reveal yourself to your agent?"

Kamal sighed. "Have you ever bought one of my books before?"

"What do you mean?"

"Have you ever bought a book that I wrote?" Kamal asked.

"This one," Tucker said, pulling out a copy of *Castle in the Field* from his messenger bag.

"What about my other books? Did you buy either of my other two books—even for this story?" Kamal said.

Tucker looked slightly flustered. "No. Why?"

"Why didn't you buy my other books?"

"Frankly, there are thousands and thousands of books that come out each year. There's no way I would be able to filter through the humungous amount of books without some curating on the part of the book-store chains," Tucker responded.

"Yeah. I feel you. Fair enough. Well, when is the

last time you bought a book by a African-American male writer—who is still alive?"

At this, Tucker became defensive. "I don't think about the race of people when I buy books. How could I possibly know the answer to that question."

"The reality, Tucker, is that the overwhelming majority of white Americans do not buy books written by people who look like me. That leaves only African Americans to buy books written by other African Americans. Well, somewhere in the 1990s, the larger publishers realized that there was a growing market for urban fiction—which was cool. Diversity in books is always a good thing. But over time, these same presses decided to do away with the novels that reflected other aspects of African-American culture, choosing instead to double down on urban books to the point where the same presses that released some of the greatest African-American novels of all time found themselves unable to market anything that did not have a scantily clad African-American woman on the cover. And it wasn't just the publishing industry that forgot how to market the diversity of blackness. The music industry forgot, too.

"The kind of stuff I was writing couldn't work commercially, simply because, as an African-American writer, I was stuck in a box on what would be acceptable from me. White people don't have that same box around them. It's no secret. White people can write in every single genre and no one ever asks whether or not such a thing would sell—not in any macro type of way," Kamal said. "By removing my name and other ethnic signifiers from my book, I took my race out of the equation. Now all you had was my book and a little homespun backstory on a pseudonym. I have done nothing that other white writers, men and women, have not done throughout the history of American publishing. Why should it matter that I did the same thing?"

Tucker nodded, as if he were actually finally seeing the point of what Kamal was talking about. "Well, you have probably heard that there are a lot of people demanding that Polar Bear refund their money for the books that they've purchased. Do you have a comment on that?"

Kamal shook his head slowly. "It shouldn't matter who wrote the book. Either the book resonates with you or it doesn't. If a person wants a refund for my book just because they learned that I was an African-American writer, then that's on them. That's their prejudice at work. Did anyone ask J.K. Rowling for their money back when they realized that she was not Robert Galbraith?"

"Well, Robert Galbraith sold only a handful of copies before the public became aware of the ruse. If the publisher had refunded the money, it would have only been for like five hundred books or so. Clearly, your situation is different," Tucker said.

"Yeah. It is, mainly because my name is Kamal Jackson and not J.K. Rowling. Her name sold those novels after the fact. Don't blame me because my pseudonym actually worked and people felt inclined to buy the book."

Tucker scribbled furiously on his legal pad. "So what do you say to those readers out there who bought your book because they fell in love with the romanticized agoraphobe you created, clearly modeled off the likes of J.D. Salinger and the like?"

"Well, I guess people like more than the fiction that is on the page. Hey, Tucker, this is the bottom line: this industry, from the top down, has always had issues with race, as have its customers. This situation should serve as a model for the ludicrousness of judging books and authors by their ethnicities. There are no African Americans selling monster amounts of books like Stephen King, John Grisham, Tom Clancy, Danielle Steele, J.K. Rowling, Dan Brown, or Suzanne Collins. That's a fact."

Tucker smiled. "Not quite."

Kamal sat up, wondering if he had missed something. "How so?"

"Well, Mr. Jackson, that might have been true until you came along and changed that."

Later that night, Kamal vowed to stay off of social media and wait for Tucker's article to run on *The City Press's* website the next day. There would be a longer piece coming out in the print edition at the end of the week. In the meantime, he did his best to not get distracted by Twitter, Facebook, or articles that loved to indulge in the erupting social media commentary that had come to frame most cultural, sociological, and political issues of the moment.

James came in to check on him and offer his support, although Kamal could tell he was still a bit peeved that all of this had happened under his nose the entire time, without so much as a hint to what was going on.

Twan even called, offering his support and understanding, making sure to keep his comments as generic as possible, likely because he, too, felt that Kamal had been a bit duplicitous in how he had carried out his plan.

The only person he had not heard from—the only person who could have probably foretold all that would happen—was Yasmin. He picked up his phone and called her number. The phone rang three times before she answered.

"Hi, Kamal," she said.

It was the first time he had heard her voice in nearly a year, and it made his heart ache with longing.

"I miss you so much," he said. "Can I see you tonight? I really need to talk to you, to apologize to you for everything that's happened. But tomorrow things are going to change. I did an interview to set the record straight."

Yasmin sighed, a slight hum lingering in her voice. "Well, I'm glad you've figured everything out. I really am. But I can't see you."

"Why not?" he asked. "Please give me a chance to make things right between us."

"Hey, I forgive you," she responded, matter of factly.

"Yasmin, I'm doing my best not to break out the knee pads here. Can we please meet up? It doesn't have to be here. It could be anywhere in The City."

"Kamal," she said, her voice a bit firmer this time. "I'm seeing someone, and I don't think that being around you right now is a good idea. What we had in the past was good, I'll admit that, but that was a year ago. I had just gotten here. I didn't know anyone, and you were good to me. But I think we've both outgrown that situation. If you really think about it, I'm sure you'll agree."

Kamal felt his heart drop down into his stomach. He wanted to crawl up into a shell and disappear into the darkness. "You're in a relationship? A committed one?" he managed to get out.

"Yes. And it's pretty serious."

"I thought you were incapable of being in a committed relationship," Kamal said weakly.

"Well, I guess I've grown to where that's no longer the case," she responded. "Hey, I didn't mean to hurt you. We just saw the world a little too differently."

"It was the book that did it, wasn't it?"

"It wasn't just the book. It was more of the fact that you failed to recognize how wonderfully brilliant you were. The only reason you did that white guy character is because you lost faith in yourself, and that's not attractive to me. I wanted to love you. I really did. But that's neither here nor there at this point."

Kamal took a deep breath. "I see."

"Well, I have to run. Maybe I'll see you around. Things don't have to be awkward between us when we run into each other, you know."

"Okay," Kamal said, unsure of what else he could say to change her mind. "Wait. You said we would run into each other again?"

"Yeah. At the wedding?"

"Whose wedding?"

"Wow," Yasmin responded. "I didn't mean for you to find out this way. I had just assumed that James told you. After all, he and Twan are moving in together down in the Art District at the end of July. Well, you might want to talk to him about it when you see him again."

"I will."

"All right. Take care. Bye."

Kamal hung up his phone. Why would James have not told him about the wedding? He had to still be upset about the Kilgore Pickens thing. Damn, it felt like Kilgore Pickens was almost single-handedly responsible for messing up his life. Well, if he were to be completely honest with himself, he had messed himself up a long time ago when he gave up on who he was to become someone (or something) he was not.

He didn't want to confront James. He would let things settle out a bit more, and then they could have a heart-to-heart, where Kamal could enthusiastically congratulate him on his pending nuptials. In the meantime, Kamal would need to start looking for another place to live by the time the summer rolled around. He had just been too caught up in his own world to really consider the lives of those around him whom he loved and cherished.

Kamal sat down in front of his computer and saw several emails from Nelson Siblings and the press people at Polar Bear. He had ignored two messages they left on his phone. He just was not ready to deal with the repercussions of the truth getting out there. He finally decided to read the emails.

The first one from Nelson expressed disappointment in the deception and requested the Kamal call him back as soon as possible to discuss how they would move forward. Kamal had expected this one. The other emails reiterated similar positions. Polar Bear was in crisis mode, and they wanted to know how he would be able to help them put out all of the fires that had arisen, namely the horrifying prospect of refunding money for books the bookstores had already reported as sold. There would already be a nice stack of books returned to the publisher anyway, as was the way the industry worked (printing too many books and then allowing bookstores to return the ones they did not sell); this, however, was different because these sold books had the ability to pay for the ones that wouldn't ever sell and allow the publishing house to still make a profit. With six hundred thousand dollars invested in Kamal, they clearly wanted to come out ahead, not in the hole. Polar Bear was probably only used to the losses that resulted from celebrity memoirs that did not sell. Kamal imagined that little bit might have been a little easier to explain to shareholders.

He then listened to the voicemails. More of the same.

He would wait and read Tucker's article before returning the phone calls.

Until then, he decided it best to turn off the lights in his room and lie down on his bed, as he tried his best to remember the nights when Yasmin shared that space with him.

2 8

"So when were you going to tell me about the wedding?" Kamal asked. He was seated at the table in the kitchen and caught James just as he emerged from his room.

James stood there awkwardly for a moment before speaking. "I was going to tell you the day the news broke about you writing as that white dude. I have to admit, Kamal, I kind of felt *a way* about that. I guess I just decided to wait and tell you when I cooled off a bit."

"I didn't realize you were upset," Kamal said.

"Yeah, I guess you could say that I still am. I mean, dude, we've lived together for nearly five years! I thought we were friends. How could you hold out on me for nearly a year on something this big? Do you not trust me? Is that it? Is this trust thing between us a one-way street with me doing all of the driving?"

"James, it's not even like that. I just got caught up in trying to keep everything under wraps after Yasmin started tripping about it. I guess she kind of got me shook up a little. I figured that I would never have the nerve to pull this thing off if I had the people closest to me ready to talk me out of it."

James nodded slowly, then walked over to the kitchen table and took a seat across from Kamal.

"If I had it to do again," Kamal said, "I would tell you everything. But I'm curious. Would you have tried to talk me out of it? Seriously?"

James shrugged. "I don't know. You didn't really give me a chance to consider it. But if I had had a chance to really think on it, I would have encouraged you to do whatever you had to do to get people to take your work seriously.

"Being an actor requires you to constantly tightrope walk without a safety net. Morgan Freeman once said that he didn't have a Plan B when it came to acting as a young man. If he had had a Plan B, he would have easily defaulted to it early in his career, and he would have never become the Oscar-winning actor that we know him as today. You can't give yourself a way out, no matter what. That's the way I look at what you did.

"I just read the article that guy Tucker wrote on you on this morning's *City Press* homepage. You must've made quite an impression on him, because it seemed like he was on your side. He said he didn't know what he would have done as a white writer facing the same dilemma, but as a writer of color, he would have probably risked it all to get his words out to the public, stigma-free.

"You had a book that no one would buy from you as an African-American writer, so rather than let the book die, you decided to do what you could to give it life. That's what we as artists have to do."

Kamal smiled. "Thanks man. I appreciate your vote of confidence."

They sat silently for awhile.

"So I guess I should have started everything this

morning with a hearty congratulations on the nup-tials!" Kamal said, extending his hand to James for him to dap.

James looked at his hand and pulled him into a bear hug.

"I'm glad we finally cleared the air around here," James said, "because it was starting to get a little funky."

Kamal laughed.

"Plus, I needed to ask you something anyway," James said.

"What's up?"

"I wanted to know if you would serve as my best man."

"I would be honored."

"Thanks." James sat back down, as did Kamal.

"So I hear you guys are moving downtown to the Art District," Kamal said.

"It's definitely on the table. Hey, I could help you look for a new roommate, though, and I can still pay on my part a little while longer, if you need me to," James responded.

"Thanks, but with all that has happened in the past year or so, I think I might be ready to leave The City."

"Really? Where would you go?"

Kamal considered the question for a moment. "I don't know. I might go back down South and see if I can find a teaching job or something. If they don't take back my book advance, I might be able to live decently for a while down there."

"So how is that looking?" James asked.

"It's up in the air right now," Kamal responded. "I have to call my editor this morning and see what the company will decide to do about it."

James rose to his feet, yawned, and stretched his

arms toward the ceiling. "Well, hopefully they will read that Tucker kid's article first."

Kamal nodded his head. "Yeah, me, too.

---

NELSON SIBLINGS SPENT LESS THAN TWENTY seconds on the phone with Kamal, immediately asking if Kamal was available to come to their office that morning. Kamal agreed, and within an hour he was taking an elevator up one of the skyscrapers in midtown. When he got off the elevator, he wandered down the hall towards the Carson Matthews Literary Agency. For as much money as he had made them, he had never set foot in their offices.

Once he checked in with the receptionist, he was quickly escorted by one of the interns to a large conference room, where he was met a few moments later by Nelson Siblings and Carson Matthews.

"Glad you could come on such short notice," Carson Matthews said. Kamal had never heard Carson's voice before and was surprised at how high pitched and lispy that it was. Just by the fact that it was Carson speaking and not Nelson made the gravity of the situation that much more pronounced.

"No problem."

Kamal had planned to say very little and to just hear out what they had to say. Their interests were directly intertwined with his own, so he figured they would be working on something to salvage the situation. While he was unsure if Carson would have to return his agency fee along with the balance of the six hundred thousand dollars Kamal had collected, he figured that they would probably end up taking a loss with regard to that fifteen percent. The alternative would be that everyone returned his portion of the money and Carson end up suing him to get the agency fee off the returned advance. Hell, he didn't know. Sometimes he wished he had just gone to law school. Maybe then he would have an aptitude for thinking things through a bit more efficiently.

Carson dived right into the conversation.

"Everybody on our editorial team read the write up of you on the *City Press* website this morning. I have to be honest. I was unsure of how we were going to deal with you as a client when all of this went south, but reading that article gave me an idea."

"What's that?" Kamal responded.

"I have a gut feeling that you are likely to see a boost in your book sales once this story gets circulated. Yeah, there are people who are calling for your head, but when you think about it, it's all just publicity for selling the book. Our interests are directly aligned with yours, and we want you to sell as many books as you possibly can. The funny thing is, if I'm right, Vanessa Travont will get a boost in your other two books as well, as people scramble to read your other works. We are going to stick with the spin you've put on things, and I'm pretty sure we will weather this storm all right."

Kamal liked that Carson continued to use the word "we." The gravy train would apparently continue to run, which, at least for the moment, was a relief.

"Oh, yeah, and we just sold the Portuguese, Spanish, and French rights to your book. You'll be getting a check in the mail soon."

Kamal nodded. He didn't know what to think now. He enjoyed the idea of being financially comfortable, but he had gotten his money by shucking and jiving, and now that the gig was up, people were content to see him perform the role of literary minstrel. It was actually the opposite of what he had envisioned for himself when he began writing under the name Kilgore Pickens. There was supposed to be no gimmick. It was supposed to be all about the story. Now it was about him and his desire to masquerade as an obscure, older white writer. That was a story. Hell, that was *the* story.

He wished he could go back in time and ask Paul Laurence Dunbar what to do if the white public learned of the mask you were wearing and paid you to continue wearing it, although you were not fooling anyone.

Before he left the conference room, other members of the editorial team, publicity, marketing, advertising, and even subsidiary rights departments came by to meet him and congratulate him on his success. Some of the younger employees took pictures with Kamal on their cell phones and started tweeting under a hashtag put together by the marketing department, which they hoped would trend for a while on Twitter.

Kamal did not know if this was a dream or something more akin to a nightmare.

He left the building two hours later, exhausted and more unsure of himself than he had been in quite some time. He was famous now, for all the wrong reasons.

But dammit, it was a good book, Kamal thought. If people buy the book off this publicity bullshit, so be it. At least they will get a chance to read the book and make a decision for themselves. Yes, it was optimistic thinking, but what else did he have? He was unquestionably the flavor du jour, and as he headed back home, he could swear that he heard the loud ticking of the fifteen minutes of fame Andy Warhol had talk about decades earlier.

## 29

With James and Twan moving, not only would Kamal need to find a new place to live, but so would Yasmin. In the time since they ended whatever it was they had had a year earlier, Yasmin had taken to performing gigs with her "side" group full-time, leaving behind her job in the house band at Louie's. This was a big move for her. She was now making her living with Invisible People as their lead female vocalist. Kamal had gone to their website and even joined their email list. He owned both of their EPs, and while he had never worn it, he did own a purple t-shirt with the Invisible People logo across the front and the URL for the group's website on the back.

He missed her a lot these days. There was a dull ache in his chest that was once filled by being around Yasmin. He had allowed himself to completely and totally fall in love with her, to fall victim to all of those wonderful things about her: her wittiness, her lips, her eyes, her smile, her passion, her voice, her sexual prowess, and the friendship that she provided him. The one thing he could not fall in love with—simply because, apparently, it had not been there at any real point in the first place—was the way that she loved him. It was the missing ingredient from it all. It was the one reminder that, although it had been a wonderful time, those six plus months, not every memory of the history of their relationship would be a shared one. The idea that he was so completely and totally into the relationship and that she was holding a critical piece of her emotional commitment away from him, more than arms length at bay, made the situation sting. Prior to Yasmin, there had been a few others, but never as serious as what he had with Yasmin. He felt their relationship had the ability to transcend the simple girlfriend/boyfriend category. There was no ceiling in his mind for what they could have become.

She would have been the perfect reason to stay in The City. She would have helped him see his way through the Kilgore Pickens situation and offer him support as he struggled to once again find himself as an artist. Now, though, he would have to do those things alone.

He definitely did not need to remain in The City, not with the absorbent cost of living. Although he had the financial resources to live moderately on his own, he still possessed a Southern mentality, which meant that there was just so much that person was supposed to spend on his dwelling, food, or gas. The City's prices were in a bubble to themselves, completely divorced from the realities that existed elsewhere in the country.

With no fixed source of income, Kamal knew he had to be smart with his money. Staying in The City just wasn't the right move any longer. He didn't know where he would go, but he was beginning to sense it would be far away from here.

THE PUBLISHING INDUSTRY NORMALLY WENT TO sleep just before Thanksgiving and did not wake up until the beginning of February. With so many holidays and scores of publishing employees taking every other day off for vacations, personal days, or sick days, there was never really anyone in the offices.

January was drawing to a close, and it appeared there would be no further repercussions—at least from a legal point of view— from the Kilgore Pickens book. In fact, social media largely sided with Kamal and co-opted him as a poster guy for the #DiverseBooks campaign.

"If the playing field were level, Kamal Jackson would have never had to go and concoct the character of Kilgore Pickens to find a way to capture the larger American imagination," one person had commented in a blog entry that went viral.

Kamal didn't see himself as a hero, though. Those who fought on the frontline for change were the real heroes. He was just a person who had conducted an experiment that was wildly successful, in spite of the fact that his experiment's success relied heavily on the publishing industry revealing itself to be a largely prejudiced enterprise, albeit one that wanted to change and was probably looking desperately for a financial incentive to do so.

He would be "the man" over at Polar Bear a little longer, but the reality was that the book publishing industry, not unlike the music recording industry and the motion picture industry, was a fickle thing; there would always be the next big thing coming down the pipeline. Once hoopla around *Castle in the Field* died down, several months would pass, and then Polar Bear would release the paperback, and the machine of publicity would kick back up again, bringing in a second round, this one slightly smaller, of literary acclaim.

Kamal had not promoted the first edition of the book and had no plans to promote the paperback. In fact, he had no plans to even be in The City when the paperback was released. He would be somewhere far away by then, although he no idea of where that would be.

He opted not to renew his teaching contract back in the fall after the first installment of his advance had come through, and as a result, he was earning his entire income from his book. He had, of course, concealed this bit of information from James while everything was still going on. He also had been very careful with his spending, fearful that he might have to give back a portion of the money one day. After learning he would be able to hold on to the entire advance and not lose his royalties to legal judgments filed by white readers unable to accept that their new favorite book was written by a young African-American guy who had attended a historically black college and had voted, enthusiastically, for President Barak Obama—twice—he began to breathe a sigh of relief. The one lawsuit that got filed against him was dismissed by the judge on the grounds that the case had no real merit, given the history of the publishing industry, and that she did not want to clog the Court's schedule with something that was a textbook example of *de minimis*.

Kamal thought about going to visit with his mother in England for a few months while he planned his next step. It had been a while since he had seen her, and he was unsure if she was at all aware of any of the hoopla surrounding his book. She didn't like the Internet or social media, so she was rarely aware of any news that did not first appear in print.

"Hi, Mom," he said, cradling his phone against his shoulder and ear.

"Kamal! How are you, baby!"

"I'm doing fine. I don't know if you've heard about it, but your baby boy has been in the news a lot lately —at least here in The City."

"Oh, I've been following everything closely. They've been talking about it here,too. Are you okay?"

Kamal smiled. "Yes, ma'am. I'm fine."

"I know you did what you had to do."

She didn't have to say it—that was not his mother's style—but it felt good that she did. He partly expected her to make a big deal about it and question his intentions—not unlike what Yasmin had done, but knowing his mother had his back, no matter how far away she was geographically, filled him with a huge sigh of relief. "Thank you" was all he could manage.

"So when are you coming to see me?"

Her desire to move the conversation along to more pressing things made Kamal smile. "Well, actually that's kind of what I was calling about. James is finally marrying Twan, and I'll be looking for a new place soon."

"Tell them I said congratulations!"

The one time Kamal's mother had met James, she was so taken with him that she would include extra goodies in her occasional care packages to Kamal that he was instructed to share with his roommate.

"I will," Kamal said. "I'm thinking about leaving The City and moving somewhere else. I haven't figured out where just yet. I was hoping I could come and visit you for a little while, just until I can get my thoughts together."

"Well, you already know you're welcome here."

"It'll be in June, shortly after the wedding."

"Good. You can use my guest cottage out back. That way you can have a little space to yourself, if you need it. I think you'd love it here."

Kamal pondered the idea for a moment. He had only been to visit his mother a handful of times, but never for longer than two days, choosing to seek out the night life and attractions in London instead. Back then, his soul was restless, but the past year and half had slowed him down considerably. Maybe Worcestershire was a place he could live. He wouldn't know unless he tried. "I can't wait to see you," he finally said.

"I can't wait to see you either," his mother responded.

They chatted for another fifteen minutes about miscellaneous stuff going on in each country before ending their phone call with "I love yous" and promises to talk soon.

Kamal closed his eyes and allowed himself drift off, trying not to think of any of the many things circling his head.

## 30

Kamal had not expected the phone call, and when he received it, he considered rubbing everything in her face, but there was a part of him that had been severely humbled by all that had happened, so he decided to quietly hear her out.

"I just wanted to congratulate you on *Castle in the Field*," Vanessa Travont said.

"Thank you."

After that, she never mentioned the book throughout the rest of their conversation. Kamal didn't know whether that was because she had missed making a once in a lifetime killing off of the book (at least in her mind) or if she realized just how expendable she had been in Kamal's professional life. The irony, though, was that she had been the one to terminate their professional relationship, not him. In a way, he figured, she had actually helped him out. After all, she had set in motion the sequence of events that would lead to his needing to do what he did. He could have mentioned any one of these things to her, but he didn't see the point in gloating. They both knew how things had turned out.

"I see that you have the number one book in the

African-American literary fiction section of Amazon," she said.

"Which book? *Junkyard of Absurdities* or *Dope Revolution*?"

"Neither. You don't remember the novella you wrote?" Vanessa Travont asked.

Truthfully, he did not. Any thoughts of that book had been overshadowed by the Kilgore Pickens project.

"It's actually selling? I just kind of put it up there and walked away from it to deal with—other things, you know," he responded.

"Uh huh," she said, softly absorbing the blow of his comment, a tiny bit of shade tossed her way, shade, he figured, she should have expected since she was calling him after all this time. "Well, I had an editor from Stalling reach out to me and ask if you would be interested in doing a print version of the book. They would like to get both the hardback and paperback rights, and if you were willing to part with them, the electronic rights."

"Why did they not just contact me directly? I'm sure you told them that you were no longer representing me on any of my projects, right?" Kamal said.

"Okay," she responded, "I deserve that. But let's be honest here. When it comes to the books that you've written under your own name, I have done well by you. I'm sure they reached out to me because my relationship with them is still strong.

"I know you're represented by the Carson Matthews Literary Agency now on your other projects, but I'm much better at representing you in this kind of market. And I'm not going to lie to you; I'm very interested in continuing to work with you on projects that you do under your own name."

It was a bold confession, one that took away any

ability on her part to seem disinterested should he decline her invitation. In that moment, he begrudgingly respected her for that. It is one thing to say a person needed to eat crow to make everything right, but it was rare to witness them do it so humbly.

"I appreciate the offer, but I remember that last book signing and how you ignored it, even though it was in your own neighborhood, and how you called me into your office on a Sunday to hand me my walking papers. I remember feeling like you really didn't care about me as a person. I was depressed for weeks after that. You yanked away the one thing that made me happy and did it so coldly and unapologetically. I'm not sure I could ever trust you at this point."

Kamal wanted to clear the air. He wanted to make sure that if this was going to be the last time they spoke, he had at least unburdened himself of the pain he felt and given himself a moment of transference, where that bit of negative energy that had sat upon his chest, even while he was going through the Kilgore Pickens project, was now released onto Vanessa Travont for her to deal with.

"I'm giving you your apology now," she responded. " I can't take back what I did. And, yes, I was wrong about the way I handled everything, but I wouldn't be coming back to you, hat in hand, if I didn't feel that there was something I could genuinely contribute to your writing life."

"How much?"

"What do you mean?" she asked.

"How much is Stallings Press offering?" Kamal said.

"Twenty-five thousand dollars for the advance and the usual on royalties."

"Twenty-five thousand dollars for one novella?"

"Yes."

"They must be pretty desperate to get their hands on it then," Kamal said.

"It appears that way," Vanessa Travont said.

"Well, let me look over my ebook accounts and see what my sales actually are, and I will call you back if I am interested in doing a deal with them. Is that cool?"

"That's fine," she responded. "Just let me know—either way."

"I will. And Vanessa?"

"Yes."

"I just wanted let you know that I appreciate your call. In the beginning we had some really good times. Maybe we can get those back one day."

"That would be nice," she said, before hanging up.

Kamal logged onto his various accounts and began the task of pouring over his sales from the past three months to see what exactly the fuss was over.

His eyes grew large when he saw the numbers. He hadn't expected to sell anything online, but he'd managed to sell over twenty-five thousand copies of his book in less than a month alone. It was then that he realized that Stallings Press was trying to romance his book out from under him by offering him what looked like a large advance. He had made well over that amount since he had self-published the book and could not see the logic in taking a micro royalty in comparison to the money he was receiving each month from Amazon, Kobo, Barnes & Noble, iBookstore, and Google Play.

Still, he promised himself he would follow up with Vanessa Travont. If Stalling wanted that book, they would have to pay a lot more than they were offering, and he was unsure if that was even possible.

He picked up the phone and called Vanessa.

Patiently, he went over the numbers with her.

"I can't believe it," she finally said. "Those are your actual sales so far?"

"Yes. I'm reading directly from the screen in front of me, no filler," he responded.

"Well, this is a first."

"What do you mean?"

"Oh, I mean it's a first for me telling someone that they don't need me," Vanessa Travont said.

"What do you mean?"

"I can't, in good conscious, even recommend you sign with anyone at this point. They couldn't offer you an advance that would get your attention, and they probably wouldn't go beyond their current offer for a novella. They know that the industry doesn't sell novellas well, and, personally, I believe they were taking a risk with the offer that they made. Now, paying substantially more than that would get us laughed out of there, even with them having knowledge of your real numbers. And since I can't close a deal with them, you don't really need me at this point," she said.

Kamal was quiet for a moment. "So that's it then?" he finally said.

"For now, yes. If you decide to write another Kamal Jackson book, feel free to shoot it my way, if you would like."

"Sure thing," Kamal responded.

He hung up the phone and set it on his desk. His laptop was still open, and he found himself going to the Invisible People website and looking at tour pictures of Yasmin. Her hair was longer now, and she looked every bit a native of The City. The style of her clothing had changed, and she had developed a swag that was pretty much a natural extension of her usual style, only slightly amplified. She was starting to take on the aura of someone famous, someone that Kamal could scarcely recognize.

I used to love her, he thought, suddenly remembering Common's personified ode to hip hop. But she was happy now, happy enough to commit herself to this new guy. This was something he had been unable to achieve, and there was a part of him that wanted to ask that guy what his secret had been. How did he get Yasmin to do something that Kamal had struggled and ultimately come up short attempting to do?

Kamal imagined he was well overdue for dating someone new, though. It wasn't as if his libido had evaporated after Yasmin left. He had just busied himself to the point he muted out his desires most of the time.

Maybe it was just time to move on.

From everything.

Vanessa.

Yasmin.

Teaching.

Maybe even from writing—at least for a while.

## 31

James began moving his things out of the apartment a month before the wedding. Up until that moment Kamal had not really known how much stuff was in his roommate's room. While meticulously clean, the room seemed to hold the contents of a house unto itself. Not caring to take the sofa and love seat with him, James offered them to Kamal, who accepted them but knew he would likely part with them in the coming months himself now that he had opted to go to England for awhile. They made several trips back and forth to the art district to drop off James's things, but on the last trip Kamal and James ran into Twan and Yasmin, who were just beginning to move Twan's things.

"You guys need any help?" Kamal offered, trying to avoid making eye contact with Yasmin.

"No thanks," Twan responded. "I'm using movers. I'm not about to mess up my back with this stuff."

James laughed loudly. "I told you I would help you."

"No. I'm good. You get *your* stuff; I get *my* stuff. We have plenty of years for you to move things around for me."

James laughed again.

"So how have you been?" Yasmin said, poking Kamal playfully in his chest with her index finger.

"Just chillin'."

He started to say more but decided against it.

A full beat passed.

"Did you feel that?" Twan said.

"What?" James responded.

"That cool breeze that came down through here just now. Maybe we should leave these two to catch up privately. Plus, I want to show you this coffee shop on the corner that has me about ready to lose my mind."

James and Twan walked out the apartment, as if they were the visitors and not Kamal and Yasmin.

"Congrats on your stuff with The Invisible People," Kamal offered.

"Thank you. I'm glad that things have picked up. We're traveling a lot these days."

"Yeah, I noticed your tour schedule on your website."

"You've been following us?" she asked.

Kamal swallowed hard and lowered his head. "You guys are one of my favorite bands."

"That's so sweet!"

"Yeah. Well, I guess."

Yasmin stepped closer to Kamal. "You know, it doesn't have be like this between us. We used to be close."

"And I used to be in love with you."

Yasmin sighed. "Dammit, Kamal. I really want to be cool with you. You must be determined to build a wall between us."

"The way I see it, if you fail me as a lover, then you fail me as a friend, too."

"Really? Wow. Okay. Fuck it. I'm through trying

with you. I just figured that we might run into each other given that Twan and James are getting married. Holidays and stuff. You're not even trying to be cordial about it." Yasmin shook her head, the frustration in her face heavy, as if on the verge of falling onto the floor in front of them.

Kamal started to tell her about his moving to England and how he was moving on with his life, but when he opened his mouth, he found that he couldn't bring himself to fight with her any longer.

"I'm sorry. I'm just still sore about things."

Yasmin stared at him for a moment, unsure if he was bating her into another argument.

"Can I just ask you a question?" he said.

"Go ahead."

"Is there anything I could've done differently to change all of this with you and me?"

Yasmin took a deep breath, not out of anger but preparation for what she would say. "Believe it or not, Kamal, the world doesn't really revolve around you like that."

"Hold up. I'm not trying to pick a fight here."

"I'm not being mean. I'm just being real. I just don't see you as someone I would want to be in a committed relationship with. I don't do relationships well. You were always much safer not being my boyfriend."

"What does that even mean?" he asked.

"Relationships are about obligations and compromises. Some people are built to love in spite of those things, but not me. As my friend, I can always have you in my life. In a relationship, you'd just be a boyfriend who got discarded along the way."

Kamal shook his head, trying to comprehend her logic. "But you have a boyfriend now."

"No. I don't. I *had* a boyfriend—which proves my point."

"I guess we just see the world differently. I want someone in my life I can build with."

"And you deserve that."

"I thought I had that with you."

To this Yasmin didn't respond.

"The best I could ever be to you is a friend," she said, "but until you can see the advantage of being in my life like that, I guess I'll have to accept things the way they are."

"I don't know if I could be your friend without having feelings for you," Kamal said.

"I have feelings, too. I just choose to deal with them differently."

"I would want to kiss you and hold you in my arms, and I don't need that kind of temptation in my life."

"We could be friends and still share intimate moments," she said.

"But it wouldn't be going anywhere," Kamal added.

"No. It would actually be going everywhere. If you were my friend, you would always be my friend, which is more than either of us could say for any relationship we'd ever enter into."

Kamal was unsure if he agreed—or even understood.

"I'm leaving after the wedding. Moving to England," he blurted out.

"Okay. And?"

He didn't know why he said it. Maybe he wanted to suggest that he couldn't be her friend because he was moving to another continent, but that didn't make any sense in the age of Internet technology.

"If you're ever in England, look me up."

"Okay. And if you're ever in The City, you can look me up," Yasmin responded matter-of-factly.

"Yeah."

"Yeah."

They stood there awkwardly for a moment trying not to look at each other.

"Care for some coffee?" Kamal finally said.

"I could go for that."

They locked the door behind themselves.

*B-Sides and Remixes*

*30 Love: A Novel*

*Mojo's Guitar: A Novel (Il était une fois Morris Jones)*

*Afro Nerd in Love: A Novella*

*The Keys of My Soul: A Novel*

*The Race of Races: A Novel*

*The Illest: A Novella*

*Bessie, Bop, or Bach: Collected Stories*

*Four Floors (with Sabin Prentis)*

*Black Hand Side: Stories*

*White Pages: A Novel*

*She Lives in My Lap*

*Reverb*

*Work-In-Progress*

*Daykeeper*

*Most of My Heroes Don't Appear On No Stamps*

*Portable Black Magic*

# ACKNOWLEDGMENTS

I would like to give a special thanks to my brother, Torrey; my sister-in-law Sarah; my sister-in-law Brandi; my partner-in-writing, Sabin; and my wife, Lauren.

Also, I would like to thank my daughter, Zoë, who will one day read this and understand a little more about how her daddy's imagination worked.

## ABOUT THE AUTHOR

Ran Walker is a native Mississippian who gave up the practice of law to become a writer. He is also the multi-award-winning author of seventeen books. His work has appeared in various anthologies and literary journals, and he was awarded several fellowships, including the Mississippi Arts Commission/National Endowment for the Arts Fellowship for Creative Nonfiction in 2005. He has participated in both the Hurston-Wright Writers Workshop and the Callaloo Writers Workshop. He is the recipient of the National Indie Author Award, the BCALA Ebook Fiction Award, and the Virginia Indie Author Project Award.

Walker serves as a creative writing professor at Hampton University and enjoys spending his time reading, composing music, taking photographs with his iPhone, and exploring the country with his wife, Lauren, and daughter, Zoë.

He can be reached at www.ranwalker.com.

www.ingramcontent.com/pod-product-compliance
Lightning Source LLC
Chambersburg PA
CBHW070303120726
47910CB00007B/2357